THE PROBLEMS OF LOVE

The Marquis of Osminton prided himself on being the most selfish man in the *Beau Ton*, but his distant cousin, Alexia Minton surprises him into an unselfish action.

His effort is, however, unsuccessful and the Marquis is extremely irritated when his mother the Dowager Marchioness insists on making good his mistake by chaperoning Alexia and her beautiful sister, Letty.

How the Marquis finds himself with innumerable problems to solve and how, despite every resolution to remain aloof, he becomes involved, is told in this dramatic and exciting story set in Regency London.

Barbara Cartland

The Problems of Love

CORGI BOOKS
A DIVISION OF TRANSWORLD PUBLISHERS LTD

THE PROBLEMS OF LOVE

A CORGI BOOK 0 552 10804 9

First publication in Great Britain

PRINTING HISTORY
Corgi edition published 1978
Corgi edition reprinted 1982

Copyright © Barbara Cartland 1978

This book is set in 10/10½pt Times

Corgi Books are published by Transworld Publishers Ltd.,
Century House, 61-63 Uxbridge Road,
Ealing, London, W5 5SA
Made and printed in Great Britain by
Hunt Barnard Printing Ltd., Aylesbury, Bucks.

Author's Note

The descriptions of the Prince Regent's hesitation and anxiety over the Fête to celebrate his Regency are correct, and it actually took place on July 19 1811.

His passionate feelings for Lady Hertford are fully recorded, and many historians were misled by the slanderous cartoons of the period into believing that she was his mistress.

She was extremely unpopular, and during the riots which took place at the time of the Queen's trial the rioters surged round her house and broke all the windows.

However, she retained her virtue, but was exceedingly upset when she was supplanted in the Royal affections in 1820 by Lady Conyngham.

Chapter One

1811

"No!" the Marquis of Osminton said.

Imogen Harlow stamped her foot.

It was a very pretty foot but Lady Harlow's extremely pretty face was contorted in an expression of anger which made her look hard and not particularly attractive.

"How can you be so unfeeling—so selfish?" she asked.

"That is my reputation," the Marquis replied, "and I am not ashamed of it."

"Well, you should be!" she stormed. "You never think of anything or anyone except yourself!"

"I learnt a long time ago that the only time life becomes troublesome or difficult," the Marquis retorted, "is when I think of other people. When I concern myself with myself everything goes smoothly."

"Well, it is not going smoothly now," Lady Harlow snapped. "I see absolutely no reason why you cannot ask the Prince Regent to invite me to dinner just one evening. After all, you are there almost every night."

"The Prince's small dinner-parties are for his intimate friends," the Marquis explained.

"Why should I not become one?" Lady Harlow

demanded. "Or are you jealous? If you are jealous, Chilton, I am almost inclined to forgive you."

"I am not jealous for the simple reason that you know as well as I do that His Royal Highness prefers much older women. You are too young, Imogen, and that is the answer that must satisfy you for the moment. In ten years' time the Regent might find you alluring."

"I shall not be all that old in ten years' time," Imogen Harlow asserted.

A faint smile twisted the Marquis's lips.

He had known she would rise to that bait, which might for the moment take her mind off her main objective.

That was to be invited to Carlton House on the evenings when the Prince of Wales, recently appointed Regent, surrounded himself with those he considered to be his special friends and the women whom he found most attractive.

At the moment his favourite was Lady Hertford, who, over fifty years of age, had supplanted Mrs. Fitzherbert in his affections.

The Marquis, though he was not prepared to say so, had in fact not considered either the Regent's feelings or Lady Harlow's in making the decision not to promote their meeting except on formal occasions.

Although he found Imogen Harlow for the moment alluring and seductive, he was well aware, in some cool, practical part of his mind, that, like so many of his other love-affairs, she would not last long.

She had been determined he should become her lover and this had not been difficult since her husband, Sir George Harlow, disliked Society and the gaieties of London.

Instead, he spent his time on his estate in Gloucestershire, breeding cattle which won prizes at every local show.

Imogen Harlow was well aware of her good looks, and as her husband was generous where money was concerned it was easy for her to establish herself in London Society.

She was invited to Devonshire House, Bedford House, and Richmond House, where the great hostesses entertained, but the intimacy of Carlton House had so far eluded her.

Because she was determined to gain her objective she now tried a different tack.

"I thought you loved me, Chilton," she said in a plaintive, little-girl voice which most men found irresistible.

The Marquis did not reply and after a moment she went on:

"I know you have never said so in so many words, but you cannot deny that I excite you, and we have had some very, very happy moments together."

There was a touch of emotion in the last words, which the Marquis did not miss but which only made him look a little more cynical than before.

He was so used to women extorting payment for the enjoyment they afforded him if not in money then in jewels, or anything else they required, that he told himself that he had no intention of altering his decision on this matter.

He was determined to stand firm for the simple reason that he was too astute to get himself so talked about that otherwise complaisant husbands came posting back to London intent on seeking their revenge.

As far as he was concerned, while the Social World might suspect that he and Imogen were having an *affaire de coeur,* he had no intention of providing firm grounds for such suspicions.

He therefore saw her as much as suited him in private, but was extremely discreet about how often and where they appeared in public.

When he did not answer, Lady Harlow moved from the window to walk towards him as he leant back in a velvet arm-chair which seemed a fitting frame for his elegance.

The Marquis of Osminton was one of the most admired men in the whole of the *Beau Monde*.

It was not only that he was extremely handsome and dressed with an elegance that accentuated his slim, athletic figure and broad shoulders; he was also envied and acclaimed by all the younger Bucks and Dandies as a Corinthian.

There was no-one in the circle which surrounded the Prince Regent who could tool a high-perch Phaeton more swiftly and accurately, who could ride more spirited horses, or was a more accurate shot with a duelling-pistol.

"You not only command the admiration of the ladies, Chilton," the Prince had said to him once, "but, dammit, the men admire you too."

The Marquis realised there was a touch of pique and jealousy behind the Prince's remark.

He too longed to be admired, but because of his debts and his behaviour the public more often booed him than they cheered.

He had however a number of friends like the Marquis who realised and appreciated the Regent's exceptional qualities.

This was why in the past Mrs. Fitzherbert had always encouraged him and on more than one occasion had said with a sigh:

"You are such a good influence on the Prince. I only wish I could say the same of his other friends."

The Marquis, however, while admired by his contemporaries, was not always liked by them.

He was known as being a hard man, ruthless in many ways, and, as Lady Harlow had said, extremely selfish.

This was not surprising, considering he had inherited when he was young not only an ancient and respected title but also an immense fortune.

His estates were part of the grandeur of England and understandably he was very conscious of his own importance.

"Please, Chilton," Imogen Harlow said now, standing in front of him.

She was well aware as she did so that it would be impossible for him not to notice the lines of her exquisite figure under the transparent gauze of her gown.

She looked very much prettier when her eyes were soft and her red lips pouted a little in a provocative way.

The Marquis's eyes, which were dark and penetrating, seemed however to look beneath the surface as he said in an extremely uncompromising manner:

"The subject is beginning to bore me, Imogen. I have said no, and I mean no!"

With a considerable effort Lady Harlow forced the suspicion of tears into her eyes.

"Oh, Chilton," she said unhappily, and her lips turned downwards.

The Marquis laughed and it was not a particularly kindly sound.

"I am immune to tears," he said. "They leave me unmoved and usually rather irritated."

He put his arm round Lady Harlow and with his other hand lifted her chin.

"If you stop nagging me," he said, "I will give you that bracelet that you admired so much in Bond Street yesterday."

For a moment Lady Harlow struggled against an inclination to tell him he could keep the bracelet.

Then her natural greed, combined with some shrewdness, told her that further argument would only antagonise the Marquis and make it even more impossible for her to get what she wanted.

"Thank—you," she said in a little voice which would have made any other man think he was being a brute.

As she spoke she looked at the Marquis from under her eye-lashes and saw by the twist of his lips that he saw through every move of her play-acting.

It was doubtless only a repetition of a performance at which he had been the sole member of the audience a dozen times before.

Because she had no desire to antagonise the man she found not only irresistible but also a considerable feather in her cap, she flung her arms round his neck and drew his head down to hers.

"Why do we argue when there are so many delightful things we could be saying to each other?" she asked.

The Marquis kissed her without passion. Then when she would have tried to hold on to him he set himself free.

"You must leave now, Imogen," he said. "I have an appointment in half an hour and have some letters to sign first."

"I shall see you tonight?"

"I am dining with the Regent, as you know," the Marquis replied, "but if His Royal Highness does not keep me too late I will call on you on my way home."

"You know I shall be waiting; you know too how I shall be longing to see you."

The Marquis hardly listened.

It was no more than he had expected to hear, and he moved towards the door so that there was nothing Lady Harlow could do but follow him.

He escorted her through the magnificent marble Hall which was decorated with extremely fine paintings by George Stubbs of some of his father's favourite horses.

There he bowed and kissed her hand, while a footman from a long line of stalwart young flunkeys in livery hurried to open the door of the carriage waiting outside under the portico.

With punctilious politeness, for the Marquis was noted for his good manners, he waited with a slight air of impatience until the wheels of the carriage started moving.

Then he turned and walked back through the

Hall, returning not to the Salon where he had been with Lady Harlow, but into his own special room where he sat when he was alone.

It was in fact the most interesting room in the house, with the walls decorated with books and several more magnificent paintings of horses, which were the envy of the Prince Regent.

The Marquis however walked to a large desk which stood in front of the windows and sat down at it.

There were a number of papers waiting for him and as he picked up the first one he also rang a bell which stood on the desk.

The door was opened almost instantly and his Comptroller and Private Secretary came into the room.

Mr. Dugdale, who was a middle-aged man with an intelligent face, had the bearing of a soldier, which in fact he had been before he entered the Marquis's employment.

Without looking up from the letter he was reading the Marquis said:

"Send Lady Harlow some flowers and say I shall unfortunately be unable to call on her this evening."

Mr. Dugdale wrote the instructions he had just received into a note-book which he was carrying in his hand.

"And send a footman to buy the diamond bracelet that I inspected in Hunt and Roskell's in Bond Street yesterday," the Marquis went on. "They will know which one it is."

"Very good, My Lord."

Mr. Dugdale said no more, but the Marquis, knowing him so well, was aware that there was a certain stiffness in his attitude, which told him without words that he did not approve.

He knew that his Comptroller, who was more of a friend than an employee, was inclined to take a dislike to one or another of his many lady-friends and there was little doubt that he had no partiality for Lady Harlow.

7

"I know what you are thinking, Dugdale," the Marquis said in an amused tone, "and though I think it is a damned impertinence on your part, I am beginning to think you may be right."

Mr. Dugdale gave a little sigh which was quite obviously one of relief.

"I have said nothing, My Lord," he remarked after a moment.

"Curse it, but I can hear you thinking!" the Marquis replied.

He sat back in his writing-chair and turned it a little sideways so that he could look at his Secretary.

"What is the matter with women, Dugdale, that they have no originality about them? They all appear to have been cut from the same pattern."

"Perhaps, My Lord," Mr. Dugdale replied, choosing his words with care, "where you are concerned they have all come from the same source."

The Marquis considered this for a moment, then he said:

"That is certainly a reasonable explanation, but in fact I find them irritatingly predictable in their behaviour and distressingly banal in anything they have to say."

"I can only agree with you, My Lord," Mr. Dugdale said, "in the examples of womanhood to whom I imagine you are referring."

The Marquis laughed. Then he asked:

"Are you seriously suggesting that I should look further afield and in other directions?"

"Why not?" Mr. Dugdale replied. "Though the world is a large place, we are inclined to confine ourselves to a very small portion of it."

"You are right," the Marquis agreed. "And if only this damned war was over we could go abroad. Meanwhile, we are confined to this island and there is nothing we can do about it."

"Nothing, My Lord," Mr. Dugdale agreed. "And I should be grateful if you would sign your letters.

Some of them concern the Castle, and I have a groom waiting to convey them to Mr. Saunders."

This was the Marquis's Agent for his huge estate in Kent.

He pulled his chair back to the desk and without perusing the letters too closely, knowing that he could trust his Comptroller completely, affixed his signature to the bottom of each one.

When he had finished there was quite a pile of them and the Marquis looked at his watch.

"I have rather wasted the afternoon," he said, "but I think . . ."

He was interrupted as the Butler opened the door.

"What is it, Adams?"

"There's a young lady asking to see you, M'Lord. She says she has no appointment but would be greatly obliged if Your Lordship would grant her a few moments of your time."

"A young lady?" the Marquis questioned.

"Her name, M'Lord, is Miss Alexia Minton."

The Marquis raised his eye-brows and looked at his Comptroller.

"Minton?" he repeated. "And which of my many relatives can this be?"

Mr. Dugdale thought for a moment.

"I cannot place her, My Lord."

"Then go and find out who she is," the Marquis ordered.

Then as his Comptroller turned towards the door he changed his mind.

"No, let her come in, and if I need you to rescue me I will ring the bell. I usually find my relatives insufferable after about five minutes!"

Mr. Dugdale nodded to the Butler, and after he had gone, closing the door behind him, he said:

"While you are making the young lady's acquaintance, My Lord, I will look her up in the Family Tree. She certainly cannot be a near relative unless she has changed her Christian name."

9

"Do that, Dugdale," the Marquis agreed. "Quite frankly I find it difficult to summon up any particular interest in my relatives, who, thank God, have learnt over the years not to intrude upon me unnecessarily."

When Mr. Dugdale had left the room the Marquis thought he had in fact made it clear that the Mintons as a family did not interest him.

He had no intention as the head of the family of behaving either as a father-figure or as what he described to himself as a "bottomless cornucopia."

The Marquis had time only to rise from his desk, walk to the end of the room, and stand in front of the magnificent marble mantelpiece designed by Adam when the door opened and the Butler announced:

"Miss Alexia Minton, M'Lord!"

A girl came into the room moving slowly but in a manner which told the Marquis that she was nervous and a little apprehensive as she advanced towards him.

She wore a plain but attractive bonnet, trimmed simply with dark blue ribbons, and when she raised her head the Marquis could see beneath it a small oval face that seemed dominated by two large grey eyes.

When she was within a few feet of him his visitor swept him a curtsey, then stood looking at him in a manner which made him feel quite sure she intended to supplicate him in one way or another.

"You are ... the Marquis of ... Osminton?" she asked after a moment in a quiet, soft voice.

"I am," the Marquis replied, "and I understand from your name that you are one of my relatives."

"Quite a ... distant one. My grandfather was your grandfather's second cousin."

There was a little pause and after a moment the Marquis asked:

"Is that the reason why you came to see me?"

"No, not ... exactly," Alexia Minton answered, "but I thought you might be able to ... help me, and I hoped you would not think it an ... imposition."

"I cannot answer that question until you tell me what you require," the Marquis replied. "Suppose we sit down?"

He indicated a chair with a gesture of his hand and noted that Alexia sat on the edge of it, her back very straight, her hands in her lap, like a child in front of a teacher.

Her gown was plain, a little old-fashioned, the Marquis noted with an experienced eye, but in good taste, while the dark blue of the material seemed to accentuate the whiteness of her skin.

Her hair was fair, not golden but with the soft fairness of a field of corn that is not yet ripened.

Her eyes as she turned them towards him were very expressive, and he noticed that she still seemed rather nervous.

"Well?" he asked, sitting himself in a chair opposite to her and crossing his legs. "What can I do for you?"

He spoke in a more kindly tone than he usually used to strangers, simply because the girl facing him seemed so inexperienced and unsure of herself.

"My father was Colonel Arthur Minton," Alexia replied. "He died last year after a long illness. As I now have the family to look after, because my mother died five years ago, I felt it incumbent upon me to bring my sister to London."

The Marquis was listening but he made no comment.

"She is so beautiful, I felt it would be wrong," Alexia went on, "to keep her in Bedfordshire, where we are very isolated, and not to give her a chance of seeing . . . the world."

She hesitated over the last two words and the Marquis in a cynical tone said:

"What you are really saying is that you wish to give her a chance of finding a husband."

There was something scathing in his voice which brought the colour into Alexia's pale cheeks.

11

"It sounds rather ... forward, My Lord, but I felt it right to do what my mother would have done if she were alive."

"Will you explain how I come into this?" the Marquis suggested.

"I learnt when I made enquiries," Alexis replied, "that you own some furnished property in London, and it was actually your Agent who suggested you might have a house that I could rent for the Season ... but I am afraid I could not pay very ... much for it."

The Marquis looked surprised.

He was aware he had furnished properties amongst the large residential estates that he owned in London, but such things were always left in the hands of one of his Agents.

He was also aware that it was ignorance on Alexia's part and not, as he might have expected from someone else, a desire to ingratiate herself which had brought her directly to him.

"Are you suggesting that you should set yourself and your sister up in a furnished house without a Chaperon?" he asked after a moment.

"I ... thought," Alexia answered, "that as I am so much ... older than Letty I might be sufficient Chaperon if we had our Governess living in the house. She now teaches my small brother."

"So there are three of you!" the Marquis exclaimed. "I can assure you, Miss Minton—or since we are cousins may I call you Alexia?—the Social World, to which you obviously aspire, would not consider you a proper Chaperon for a débutante."

"Are you ... sure of ... that?" Alexia asked anxiously.

"I am stating a fact," the Marquis replied. "How old are you that you can think of yourself in such a capacity?"

Alexia hesitated and he knew from the expression in her eyes that she wanted to lie to him. Then after what he was sure was a tussle with her conscience she told the truth.

"I am nearly twenty-one," she said, "but I thought if I said I was twenty-four or twenty-five no-one would be . . . able to check on it."

The Marquis smiled.

"I think you would find it hard to find anyone who would believe you have reached such an august age," he said. "But apart from that, you are unmarried."

Alexia sighed.

"I was afraid that might be an obstacle," she said despondently, then with a sudden light in her eyes she asked:

"Do you think that I . . . ?"

The Marquis shook his head.

"I am not being rude, or obstructive, Alexia, when I tell you that a ring on your finger will not make you look like a married woman."

He knew she could not follow his reasoning.

At the same time, he told himself that she looked so young, innocent, and unsophisticated that only the actual presence of a genuine husband would convince anyone that she was married.

There was silence. Then after a moment Alexia asked:

"Would a Chaperon . . . if I could find one, be very . . . expensive?"

"I gather from that remark that your funds are somewhat limited," the Marquis said.

"I have been saving up for two years for this," Alexia replied, "ever since I realised how beautiful Letty was going to be. Papa and I knew she was very pretty, but now she has blossomed into such a beauty that I feel she has only to be seen for . . ."

Alexia's voice died away and she looked at the Marquis a little helplessly as she said:

"I did not realise there would be so many difficulties. I thought at first we could stay at an Hotel, but they are very expensive, and last night men . . . looked at Letty in a way I did not . . . like."

"An Hotel is certainly not a place from which to launch a débutante," the Marquis said positively.

13

"Then do you think you have a house . . . quite a small one . . . that we could rent for the next two months?" Alexia asked.

"And what about the Chaperon?" the Marquis enquired.

Alexia made a little helpless gesture with her hands as she said:

"Perhaps . . . you know of . . . someone amongst your many acquaintances who would accept . . ."

Again she paused and the Marquis realised she was calculating before she finished the sentence: "Twenty-five pounds, or thirty."

He thought it very unlikely that a Lady of Consequence would think this sufficient for her services.

Vaguely at the back of his mind he knew that some London hostesses took upon themselves to introduce young girls into Society.

Usually they were bringing out a daughter of their own, and the fact that there was any monetary transaction about it was a discreet secret which would never be divulged openly.

He told himself that the whole idea was hopeless and would certainly be unsuccessful.

All he had to do was to tell Alexia he could not help her and leave her to sort out her problems in her own way.

Then he thought he might as well do the generous thing in telling Dugdale to put her in touch with his Agent, and was just about to suggest it when Alexia asked:

"Would you like to see Letty? I brought her with me but asked your Butler to put her in another room while I talked to you."

"Why did you do that?" the Marquis asked.

Alexia's eyes met his for a moment, then she answered:

"I was afraid you might think it . . . impertinent of me coming to you when our relationship is so distant, and if you were angry it would be best for Letty not to be . . . upset by it."

"While you were strong enough to bear such treatment, I suppose," the Marquis said dryly.

"I have to think of my family," Alexia answered. "As I have already said, there is no-one else."

"We have quite a number of relatives between us," the Marquis remarked.

"If we have they have never bothered themselves with us. We had one or two cousins who used to come and stay at Christmastime because Mama was sorry for them; but now they are very old or dead, and Bedfordshire is not a County which attracts rich or sporting people."

"Why do you live there?" the Marquis asked.

"Papa was left a house by a man who had served with him in India. I think Papa saved his life. He never married and therefore when he died he left Papa his house and what money he had. It was very little."

"And your father had no money?"

"Only his pension, but that died with him. Mama had a small dowry, but I am afraid we have had to spend most of that."

Alexia looked at the Marquis as if she begged him to understand that she had not been extravagant.

"Do you think that the expense of a London Season for your sister is really justified in the circumstances?" the Marquis asked after a moment.

He saw that Alexia considered his question before with a sudden smile which seemed to illuminate her face she said:

"May I fetch Letty, My Lord? Then perhaps you can judge for yourself whether I am justified in what I am planning or not."

Without waiting for his permission she sprang to her feet.

Because the Marquis could think of no good reason why he should not see the girl, he said nothing as Alexia half-ran across the room and pulled open the door.

She obviously did not realise it would have been more conventional if a servant had fetched her sister.

15

Barbara Cartland

Alone, the Marquis sat back with his usual cynical expression on his face.

He was quite sure that Letty would be a pretty girl, but certainly not sensational enough to interest the blasé gentlemen of the *Beau Monde*.

The whole idea of coming to London without enough money, without a Chaperon, without a house, was so foolish that only someone half-witted or completely unsophisticated would have thought up such a plan.

And yet for some reason he did not analyse he knew he would find it difficult to quench Alexia's hopes and send her back to Bedfordshire, which was in fact the only sensible thing to do.

He had, however, little time to think before there was the patter of feet outside and Alexia came back into the room, drawing her sister by the hand.

The Marquis saw at a glance that the younger girl was dressed more fashionably and certainly more expensively than Alexia.

Her high-crowned bonnet was trimmed with flowers and her gown of white muslin was decorated with pale pink ribbons that matched the roses on it.

Alexia seemed almost to pull her across the room towards the Marquis, and as he rose slowly to his feet and Letty curtseyed he found himself looking at one of the most sensationally beautiful faces he had ever seen in his life.

There was no doubt, he told himself, that Alexia had not exaggerated. Letty was in fact an English beauty such as had been extolled in poetry and prose since the beginning of time.

Her complexion was flawless, her hair was the shining gold of the sun, and her eyes the blue of forget-me-nots.

She had a small straight nose and a pointed chin, and the Marquis's experienced eye saw that her figure was perfect, that of a young goddess.

He found himself staring at her from sheer as-

16

tonishment, and knew that Alexia watching his face was aware of it and was delighted.

If he was surprised by Letty, she was looking at him in unmistakable admiration.

Finally she exclaimed:

"You are exactly as I thought a Marquis would look! Before we came to London Alexia said I might be disappointed."

"Then I am glad I have not disappointed you," the Marquis said. "Suppose we sit down?"

Letty seated herself in the chair that her sister had recently vacated and Alexia sat near her.

They faced the window and the Marquis saw in the revealing light that Letty's beauty was in fact flawless.

Because they were obviously waiting for him to speak he said after a moment:

"Your sister tells me she wishes to introduce you to the Social World. Do you think you will find it enjoyable?"

"It will be lovely to go to Balls," Letty answered. "I love dancing!"

"There is very little chance of her doing that in Bedfordshire," Alexia interposed.

The Marquis was wondering if it would prove any easier in London with no-one to introduce them.

At the back of his mind a voice that had always guided his actions told him that, however beautiful this girl was, there was no point in his being involved.

He would get Dugdale to give them the name of his Agent, then forget about them.

At the same time, there was no doubt that Alexia had not exaggerated the charms of her sister, and he could not help feeling it would be almost a crime to let such a beauty blossom unseen.

With an effort at self-preservation which over the years had saved him from being involved in a great many things which might have spelt trouble, he said:

"I am going to send for my Comptroller, Mr.

Dugdale. He will doubtless be able to help you find some sort of accommodation. But a Chaperon is a different matter."

"Will he know of one?" Alexia asked.

"A Chaperon?" Letty questioned. "But Alexia always looks after me."

"And that is what I thought I could go on doing," Alexia answered, "but His Lordship says I am not old enough and we need a married woman."

Letty looked puzzled.

"But we do not know anyone in London."

"That is the whole point," the Marquis said, "but we will see what Mr. Dugdale has to say about it."

He rose to ring the bell on his desk and his Comptroller entered the room so quickly that the Marquis was aware that he was expecting the summons.

"We have a problem here, Dugdale," he said, "but first let me introduce you."

He turned to Alexia and said:

"This is someone who will help you—my Comptroller, of whom I have already spoken."

Alexia curtseyed and held out her hand.

"I will do my best to be of assistance," Mr. Dugdale said politely.

"This is her younger sister," the Marquis said. "Miss Letty Minton."

He was watching his Comptroller as he spoke and with a sense of amusement realised he was as astonished by Letty's beauty as he had been himself.

Then as she rose from her curtsey Letty said impulsively:

"Oh, please, if you are going to find us a Chaperon, do not find an old and grumpy one who would find fault with everything I do. The ladies in Bedfordshire look down their noses at me in such a disapproving fashion!"

The Marquis thought he could understand the reason for this, but was aware that his Comptroller was looking at him questioningly as he asked almost incredulously:

The Problems of Love

"A Chaperon?"

"That is what my cousins require, Dugdale," the
Marquis said. "First a furnished house that must be
cheap, and secondly someone who will present them
both to the *Beau Monde*. What is more, they cannot
afford to pay more than very little for the former and
practically nothing for the latter!"

He thought as he spoke that Alexia looked at him
reproachfully, as if she thought that twenty-five or
thirty pounds should certainly not be described as
"practically nothing."

But for the moment he was amused by Mr. Dugdale's astonishment that he should concern himself
with something so completely outside his usual interests.

"Furnished accommodation should not be difficult," he said slowly after a moment, "but a Chaperon
—I have no idea where to look for one, My Lord!"

"I have never known you to fail in anything I
have asked of you," the Marquis answered. "In fact
I believe you pride yourself at never being at a loss.
This is a challenge! Let us see how you rise to it!"

Mr. Dugdale put his hand to his forehead in a gesture of perplexity.

At the same time, his eyes were twinkling, as if
he realised that the Marquis was deliberately baiting
him into producing a solution to the problem.

He turned to Alexia.

"How soon will you require these things, Miss
Minton?" he asked.

"Now, immediately!" Alexia answered. "As I was
saying, I do not like the Hotel where we stayed last
night, and it is very expensive, far more so that I expected."

"Surely your and your sister are not staying alone
in an Hotel?" Mr. Dugdale asked.

Alexia smiled at him.

"His Lordship thinks I am very foolish, but I am
not as stupid as that. No, our Governess is with us and
also my brother."

19

"How old is he?" Mr. Dugdale asked with a note of relief in his voice.

"Peter is seven," Alexia replied.

Mr. Dugdale looked at the Marquis again helplessly. Then as he saw the smile on his employer's lips he said:

"I cannot think, My Lord, for the moment . . ."

The Marquis interrupted him.

"What about that relation who is always writing to me on one subject or another?" he asked. "She might be pleased to oblige me in the hope of future favours."

He spoke in a sarcastic manner which made Alexia look at him apprehensively.

The worried expression on Mr. Dugdale's face seemed to clear.

"You mean the Honourable Mrs. Featherstone," he said. "She is certainly a possibility. I imagine half the reason why she is so voluble on paper is that she has nothing else to do."

"I suggest you get in touch with her, Dugdale, and of course the finding of a furnished house for the next two months should not be difficult."

"I hope your optimism is justified, My Lord."

"In your capable hands I am sure it will be!" the Marquis retorted.

The eyes of the two men met and each knew what the other was thinking.

Then, as if Mr. Dugdale accepted the burden that had been thrust upon him, he said aloud:

"I propose, My Lord, to take the Misses Minton to my offices, where we can discuss details of what is required. I believe Your Lordship has an appointment."

"Thank you, Dugdale," the Marquis replied.

The Marquis held out his hand to Letty.

"Rely on Mr. Dugdale to do everything that is necessary," he said, "and may I hope that you will have a very happy time in London and undoubtedly become the toast of the town."

20

"That would be very exciting," Letty said, "but Alexia says I am not to expect too much."

"That is wise of Alexia," the Marquis replied, "but I am sure she is being unnecessarily cautious."

He held out his hand to Alexia and found she was looking up at him with an expression of gratitude that made him feel that he might be a Knight in armour who had rescued a damsel in distress.

"Thank you ... thank you!" she said as she put her hand in his. "How can I ever show you how ... grateful I am for your ... kindness and understanding?"

"I only hope that it will turn out the way you wish," the Marquis said. "And I am sure your sister will take the town by storm!"

"I knew you thought I was exaggerating," Alexia smiled, "but I was right, was I not?"

"You were indeed!" the Marquis replied. "You are both Mintons of whom the whole family may feel justly proud."

The colour rose in Alexia's cheeks at the compliment and for a moment her grey eyes looked shy. Then she said with a little smile:

"Thank you for including me ... but it is Letty who ... matters."

She curtseyed, then followed Letty and Mr. Dugdale, who had already reached the door.

When she reached them she turned back and it seemed for a moment as if the sunshine had been caught in her eyes as she said again:

"Thank you ... thank you so very ... very ... much!"

Then the door shut behind them.

Chapter Two

The Marquis found the Regent in one of his agitated moods.

"I am glad you are here, Chilton," he said. "I want your help in a difficult decision."

The Marquis's heart sank because he was quite certain that the "difficult decision" concerned the Fête which the Regent had looked forward to holding at Carlton House immediately after the swearing-in ceremony of his Regency.

And yet, as long as his father's physicians at Windsor continued to hint that His Majesty's mind might yet be "roused from its disordered actions," a celebration of his own accession to power would be premature.

Twice he had fixed a date for his party, then felt obliged on both occasions to postpone it because of the reports from Windsor.

"What shall I do, Chilton?" he asked, looking despairingly at an invitation which he held in his hand.

"I have already told His Royal Highness," Lady Hertford interposed, "that it is three times lucky, and if he fixes a date now we shall be able to celebrate what will undoubtedly be a very auspicious occasion."

The Marquis looked at Lady Hertford and thought once again that her striking appearance belied her rather poor mind.

Very rich, beautifully dressed, formal, stately, and undoubtedly good-looking, it was not difficult to see why, though she was several years older than the Regent, she should arouse him almost to the point of madness.

The Marquis suspected that there was something in the Regent which ever since he was a young man had made him need to be dominated by an authoritative woman older than himself.

Whatever the reason, there was no doubt that he was wildly infatuated with Lady Hertford and had said to the Marquis on more than one occasion that he was the most fortunate man alive in having her in his life.

The Marquis knew that the Regent visited her every morning when she was in London and wrote to her every morning when she was not.

"Good God, she has been a grandmother for more than fourteen years!" one of the Courtiers had remarked in scathing tones, while another said she was forbidding and in his opinion altogether distasteful.

But one of the reasons, the Marquis suspected, for her ever-increasing hold over the Regent was that she held firmly to her virtue.

Few people believed this, including the cartoonists who depicted the love-affair in the most slanderous manner.

The Marquis was convinced, from what the Prince had said to him and from his own shrewd observations, that Lady Hertford while accepting the Regent's adoration had no intention of becoming his mistress.

But even she found it difficult to prevent the Prince from being so over-dramatic in his emotions that they ended in sudden and violent attacks of illness.

He had had them all his life, and those who remembered when he was first attached to Mrs. Fitzherbert recognised the symptoms all too well.

He usually ran a high fever, a racing pulse, had

a great agitation of spirits, severe spasms, and violent inflammatory attacks on the lungs.

He was intelligent enough to recognise that his mind was the main-spring of these illnesses.

"Dammit all, Chilton," he said once, "it is not surprising that these numerous causes for vexation make me seriously ill!"

Because as he grew older the causes for vexation grew more numerous the Marquis hastily sided with Lady Hertford rather than allow him to work himself into what he privately called "a tizzy" over the date of his Fête.

"I am quite sure, Sire," he said soothingly, "there will not be another postponement."

"If there is, I shall refuse to give a party at all," the Regent said petulantly.

"And that would make us all very unhappy," Lady Hertford interposed.

The Regent smiled at her and was instantly the adoring lover he longed to be.

"I would do nothing, and that is a solemn vow from the depths of my heart," he said, "to cause you a moment's distress."

"Then, Sire, do not worry any more. Choose another date and make sure in your heart that the gods will smile upon you."

She gave him her hand as she spoke and dropped a very stately curtsey which had a great deal of grace about it, despite the fact that she was as firmly corseted as the cartoonists depicted so unkindly.

"You must leave me?" the Regent asked hastily.

"I am afraid so, Sire, but we shall meet again tonight."

"I shall be counting the minutes—no, the seconds —until that moment," the Regent replied.

He escorted her to the door and the Marquis waited in the yellow Drawing-Room for his return.

When he came back, the Regent, for all his forty-eight years, looked as happy as a young boy.

"Wonderful woman—wonderful!" he murmured.

"If only I could have been married to someone like her."

There was a shadow over his exuberance at the thought of his wife, whom he hated, and the Marquis said hastily:

"You wanted to see me, Sire, regarding something urgent?"

"Something very urgent to me, Chilton," the Regent replied. "I want your opinion on several pictures that I have been offered, and I rely on your good taste not to let me make a fool of myself as I did last month."

The Regent's own taste was in fact exceedingly good, but he was the natural prey of every sharper in the business.

The previous month he would have paid a quite considerable amount of money for what the Marquis declared the moment he saw it to be a fake.

Other experts were called in and the Marquis was proved to be right, which contributed to the very high estimation the Regent already had of his knowledge where pictures were concerned.

"I shall be very glad to advise you, Sire," the Marquis replied, "at the same time it is very seldom that you are deceived."

"That is what I like to believe," the Regent said, "but we are none of us infallible."

"None indeed, Sire," the Marquis agreed.

He was just about to leave the room when the Regent saw that Lady Hertford had dropped beside the chair in which she had been sitting a small lace-edged handkerchief.

He picked it up and held it to his lips.

"Isabella's," he explained quite unnecessarily to the Marquis. "I will wear it next to my heart, for that is where she belongs."

The Marquis did not reply, and the Regent, as if he thought he had been over-dramatic, said:

"I cannot imagine, Chilton, why with all your opportunities you remain so cynical and have, as far as I can ascertain, never really lost your heart to any woman."

"I think perhaps that unlike you, Sire," the Marquis smiled, "I am too selfish to entrust my deepest feelings to anyone except myself."

The Regent laughed, but after a moment said quite seriously:

"I still think it is extraordinary: here you are, one of the handsomest men in the *Beau Monde,* with practically every Fair Charmer waiting to fall into your arms, while you regard them, so they tell me, as if they were beneath your condescension."

"Not entirely, Sire," the Marquis replied, thinking of how many women there were to whom he had made love.

As if the Regent read his thoughts he said sharply:

"You know exactly what I am trying to say, Chilton. The women in your life are easily expendable, and when you are bored with one you pick up another as if they were pretty flowers that are only expected to bloom for a short time."

"That expresses it most eloquently, Sire," the Marquis said. "I like variety."

"Because I am so fond of you," the Regent continued, "I would like to think of you as being in love, really in love, as I am."

The Marquis repressed the desire to say that he hoped fervently that such a ghastly fate would never befall him, and aloud he said:

"I think, Sire, it is a question of fate. Either one finds someone whom it is impossible to forget, or one continues to go on seeking."

To the Regent that seemed a very plausible explanation.

"Exactly, exactly, Chilton!" he said. "And while I have found what I have sought, and God knows I am fortunate, you continue your search like an explorer setting off into the unknown."

"You have made me feel quite adventurous, Sire,"

the Marquis replied with a smile. "Now let us find out if the labels on your pictures are evolved from some flight of fancy to make them appear more valuable than they are."

This was something, he knew, which continually happened, and the London dealers were up to every trick of the trade in trying to impress the Regent with their wares.

Later, having decided that two pictures that the Regent had been offered were worth the money asked for them while the rest were undoubtedly fakes, the Marquis left Carlton House in a good temper.

He was as fond of the Prince Regent as he could be fond of a man, and he knew how wearing the last few months had been.

The Prince longed to be in a position of power, but the King was at one moment mad at the next reverted to intervals of quiet.

In the Marquis's opinion, the doctors, who were all too obviously puzzled by his symptoms, should long ago have pronounced him incapable of attending to Government.

But because they were frightened of their positions they kept varying their opinions as to whether or not His Majesty would recover.

It was natural that the Tory Government should hold fast to the hope of the King's early recovery, because they feared that the Prince would dismiss them in favour of his Whig friends.

The indecision, the Marquis was sure, was bad for the country.

Like many of the other Peers in the House of Lords, he had been seriously disturbed when Parliament was adjourned twice the previous November.

With Napoleon's Army rampaging about on the Continent, such political manoeuvring could not continue indefinitely.

Finally, on February 11, the members of the Privy Council arrived at Carlton House for the ceremony of swearing in the Prince as Regent.

27

It had been a very impressive moment and after the oaths and declarations and signings and counter-signings had all been completed the Councillors had all knelt before the Regent to kiss his hand.

'He has certainly waited long enough for it,' the Marquis thought at the time.

He remembered how the King had always frustrated his eldest son, turning down any suggestion of active service in the Army, and not allowing him to be anything but what he became, a "Prince of Pleasure."

Driving his magnificent team of horses back towards Park Lane, the Marquis remembered that he had a luncheon appointment at White's Club in Saint James's.

But he had that morning received a letter from the country to say that his mother, the Dowager Marchioness, was coming to London.

He was surprised that she should make the journey which always tired her from her house in Surrey, but he supposed there must be an important reason for her decision.

When he arrived at Osminton House and stepped down from his Phaeton, he asked the Major Domo:

"Has Her Ladyship arrived yet?"

"Her Ladyship arrived half an hour ago, M'Lord, and is upstairs in her apartments."

One wing of the huge mansion in Park Lane was always kept ready for the Dowager Marchioness if at any time she might wish to use it, but it was in fact over a year since she had last come to London.

Finding the city noisy and overcrowded, she much preferred the quiet beauty of the country, where she had many hospitable neighbours who left her little time to feel lonely.

The Marquis had visited her at Christmas and had thought she looked a little frail. It was therefore a relief to find her in what he saw at a glance was good health.

The Dowager Marchioness had been an ac-

claimed beauty when she was young, the delight of
every portrait painter after she was married, and had
still an exquisite loveliness that was not dimmed by
old age.

Her hair was dead white and her features beneath
it were as classically clear-cut as they had been when
the Marquis's father had fallen in love with her.

Despite twenty years difference in their ages they
had been extremely happy.

Perhaps their only sadness had been that they had
only one child, which would account for the fact that
the Marquis had been spoilt from the moment his first
cry rent the air.

There was no doubt now that his mother's face
lit up at the sight of him.

"Chilton, my dearest," she said, holding out both
hands.

The Marquis kissed them before he bent to kiss
her cheek.

"I am surprised to see you here, Mama."

"I thought you would say that."

"What has happened? Why am I so honoured? I
was in fact planning to visit you as soon as the Season
is over."

"I hope you will," the Dowager Marchioness replied, "but the Queen wrote to me so despairingly that
I could not refuse to come to see her, knowing it would
be impossible for her to visit me."

"So the Queen can drag you from your solitude
while all my pleas have failed to do so," the Marquis
teased.

"I had no wish to make such a long and tiring
journey," the Dowager Marchioness answered, "but I
felt it was my duty; for, dearest, what else can one do
for someone in trouble but be sympathetic and understanding?"

She paused for a moment, then said in a low
voice:

"I was shocked, deeply shocked, to hear that His

Majesty was placed in a strait-jacket. It seems to me such *lèse-majesté*. Surely they could have contrived to control him by some other method?"

"I should have thought so," the Marquis agreed.

"No wonder the poor Queen is so desperate," the Dowager Marchioness said in her soft voice.

"Do you intend to stay with her at Windsor?" the Marquis asked.

"I really do not think I could bear the discomfort and the atmosphere of tension and misery for many hours on end," his mother answered, "and I think, dearest, that your excellent horses could convey me there quite easily and bring me back when I am ready to leave."

The Marquis laughed.

"Mama, you always were a diplomat: while conceding with one hand you keep a little back with the other. But you are right, of course you are right. It would be intolerable to have twenty-four hours on end of gloom and despondency."

"I feel very sorry for the Queen," the Dowager Marchioness insisted.

That was understandable, the Marquis considered, seeing that Her Majesty had always been close friends with his mother during the long years that she had been hereditary Lady of the Bed-Chamber.

He seated himself and said:

"Well, the Queen's loss is my gain. Need I say I am delighted to have you here?"

"And I am delighted to see you, dearest," the Dowager Marchioness replied. "You look well, and very handsome, just like your father when I first saw him."

The Marquis knew there was no higher compliment and he smiled as he said:

"Need I tell you, Mama, that you are looking even more beautiful than ever? All the "Incomparables" will have to look to their laurels now that you have come to London."

The Problems of Love

"Including Lady Harlow?" the Dowager Marchioness asked with a sly glance at her son.

"I might have known that even in the country there would be little birds to bring you tit-bits of gossip," the Marquis remarked.

"Is she very lovely?"

"No, not nearly as beautiful as you are, Mama, nor so interesting."

The Dowager Marchioness sighed.

"I am so glad. I was a little nervous."

"Nervous?" the Marquis questioned.

His mother hesitated a moment, then she said:

"I am always so afraid, my darling boy, that you will be caught by some designing woman. After all, you are not only extremely desirable in yourself, but you have so much to offer your wife."

"My wife!" the Marquis ejaculated. "Good Heavens, Mama, you need have no fears on that score! I have no intention of marrying anyone—least of all Imogen Harlow!"

"Then be a little careful," the Dowager Marchioness begged.

The Marquis looked at her sharply.

"What are you trying to say to me? Be frank with me, Mama. You know I like frankness, especially when it comes from you."

"I have heard," the Dowager Marchioness said in a low voice, "that Lady Harlow is determined to make you marry her."

"Then she must indeed be more stupid even than I had thought," the Marquis exclaimed. "She already has a husband!"

"There is such a thing as divorce!" the Dowager Marchioness replied. "In fact I have been extremely disturbed lately by the number of divorces that come before the Houses of Parliament."

She suddenly clasped her thin, sensitive fingers together.

"Oh, Chilton, promise me you will never get into

31

such a tangle or cause such a scandal in the family. I could not bear it!"

The Marquis reached out to take his mother's hand in his.

"Listen, Mama, I swear that I too have no intention of spoiling the family name or my own reputation for that matter. If Imogen Harlow causes you one moment's disquiet, then I promise you here and now not to see her again!"

"Does she really mean so little to you?"

"To tell the truth, Mama, I have just recently been finding her somewhat of a bore."

"Then I am relieved, deeply relieved," the Dowager Marchioness said. "Of course, things become exaggerated and magnified, but there have been stories of her being a very determined woman."

"A woman would have to be very determined indeed to get me up the aisle," the Marquis said. "I have just been listening to the Regent extolling the virtues of Lady Hertford, which in itself is quite enough to put one off love forever!"

"Lady Hertford!" the Dowager Marchioness exclaimed disparagingly. "She is someone for whom I have never had any admiration, and indeed I have often found her to be a tiresome woman. I simply cannot understand any man allowing his wife to be talked about in such an appalling fashion."

The Marquis had thought much the same himself.

But Lord Hertford, a dedicated Tory, was a pleasant, easy-going man, moderately successful as a politician, and also moderately successful as Master of the Horse.

What he supposed was that Lord Hertford and his son, Lord Yarmouth, found it difficult to ignore the opportunity for political influence which the Regent's infatuation presented.

The Dowager Marchioness was, however, following her own train of thought.

"I would like more than anything else, my dearest," she said now, "for you to marry a really nice girl with whom you are deeply in love."

"I am sorry to disappoint you, Mama," the Marquis answered, "but I am afraid that is unlikely to happen. Firstly because I seldom meet 'really nice' girls, and secondly because through some quirk of nature I find it impossible to fall in love in the given sense of the word."

"But, darling, why ever not?" his mother enquired. "Your father was so very much in love with me, and later I with him."

"I know, Mama, and no-one could say I had a loveless childhood or was frustrated in any way. The point is, I suppose, you have set me too high a standard! I have tried to find a wife who looks and behaves like you, but quite frankly they do not exist.

The Dowager Marchioness smiled at the compliment. At the same time, her eyes when they rested on her handsome son were wistful.

"I so want you to be happy."

"I am happy, Mama. I cannot tell you what an interesting and full life I lead. And if you are thinking that I need a woman to look after me, disabuse the thought!"

The Marquis laughed before he continued:

"I have Dugdale clacking over me like a mother-hen with one chick, and the servants that you trained so well making everything run smoothly on greased wheels which I am quite certain would all too easily be thrown out of gear by a feminine hand."

The Dowager Marchioness shook her finger at him.

"You are simply making excuses, Chilton, and you know as well as I do that sooner or later you must have an heir."

The Marquis did not reply and she said softly:

"I want, before I die, to hold your son in my arms."

"That gives me a considerable number of years

more in which to enjoy my freedom," the Marquis said, "for I assure you, Mama, you are not likely to die, not when you look as you do now."

"I do not wish to be old and become like the poor King," the Dowager Marchioness said positively, her mind returning to her reason for coming to London.

"That is something that will never happen!" the Marquis said firmly. "So stop worrying about me, Mama, in case it gives you lines on your beautiful face."

"I am much less worried at this moment than I was before I arrived," his mother said frankly.

"It was quite unnecessary, and only because you listened to tittle-tattle," the Marquis retorted severely.

It always amused him how, living in the depths of the country, the Dowager Marchioness was nevertheless aware of what was happening in the Social World.

It was seldom that she was not informed about his latest love-affairs—almost, he told himself, before they had even happened.

He did, however, know that she kept up a long and voluminous corrrespondence with her old friends, one of these being the Queen herself.

Whatever her source, the Dowager Marchioness invariably knew what was happening.

Although he thought he had been discreet where Imogen was concerned, his association with her had reached her ears and doubtless those of Sir George Harlow in the wilds of Gloucestershire.

'I will finish with her right away,' the Marquis determined in his mind, and knew it would be no hardship.

He rose to his feet.

"I would have liked to have luncheon with you, Mama," he said, "but I have a rather important meeting with two Statesmen who wish to bring a special Bill before Parliament now that they feel they have the support of the Regent. Will you forgive me, and we will dine together *tête-à-tête* this evening when we can talk undisturbed."

"That will be delightful!" the Dowager Marchioness said with a smile. "And quite frankly I would rather go to bed and rest. The roads were better than I expected, but I always find travelling, even in the well-sprung carriage you gave me, extremely fatiguing."

"Then go to bed, Mama," the Marquis said. "Have your beauty sleep, and I shall look forward eagerly and impatiently to our dinner."

He bent and kissed his mother and thought as he touched the velvet softness of her cheek that it was like kissing the petal of a flower.

He knew he loved her more than any other woman he had ever known.

He went down the staircase to find Mr. Dugdale waiting for him in the Hall.

"I have never known my mother look better, or be better informed!" he said.

His Comptroller laughed.

"Her Ladyship is always up-to-date in everything. She never ceases to surprise me!"

"And me!" the Marquis agreed. "Tell the Chef to prepare her special and favourite dishes for our dinner together and see that we have the best champagne."

"I have already done that, My Lord."

"I thought you might have," the Marquis said good-humouredly.

He walked towards the door and Mr. Dugdale moved beside him.

"If you will be back by four o'clock, My Lord, I would like to have a few words with you about the new farm buildings being erected at the Castle. They seem to be overstepping the estimates quite considerably."

"We will talk it over when I get back," the Marquis said hastily, and moved a little more quickly towards his Phaeton, which was waiting outside.

He knew that his Comptroller, once he got on the

subject of costs, could be very voluble on the matter, and he was in fact looking forward to the luncheon at his Club.

It proved even more interesting than the Marquis had expected, for the two Statesmen he had arranged to meet had invited another, who was violently against the proposed Bill.

Luncheon therefore became a spirited political debate in which the Marquis joined whole-heartedly.

Just as he gloried in his triumphs on the turf, he also enjoyed the cut and thrust of the political manoeuvrings which had accelerated now that the Regent was in power.

It was therefore almost with a feeling of exhilaration that the Marquis drove back to Park Lane, noting that he was half an hour late for his appointment with his Comptroller.

There would however still be plenty of time to discuss the new farms before his appointment to fence with a friend who was as experienced as he was himself in that ancient art.

As he stepped into his house the Marquis gave his high hat to one flunkey, his gloves to another, then turned towards the Library.

"Tell Mr. Dugdale I am here," he said to the Butler, and walked away without waiting for a reply.

The cool room with its windows opening onto the garden was a delightful contrast to the heat of the sun outside.

The Marquis stood for a moment looking at the formal flower-beds and meticulously kept lawn and thought of the gardens at Osminton Castle, which would be very beautiful at this time of the year.

They sloped down to the lake where there were black and white swans moving sedately over the silver surface, and beyond would be the Park-land with the spotted deer resting in the shade of the great oak trees.

'Why the hell does Society come to London in the summer when the country is cool and lovely?' he wondered.

He heard the door open and was just about to repeat the question aloud to Mr. Dugdale when the Butler's voice said:

"Miss Alexia Minton, M'Lord!"

The Marquis turned round.

Alexia was standing just inside the door and one glance at her told him she was as worried and nervous as when he had first seen her.

It was over three weeks since he had solved her problem and that of her beautiful sister in a manner which, as well as being ingenious, released him from further responsibility.

He had learnt from Mr. Dugdale that they were installed in a small house in Mayfair which could have been let for a considerably larger sum than Alexia had been asked to pay for it, and that Mrs. Featherstone had agreed to be their Chaperon.

After that the Marquis had ceased to remember their existence, but now it struck him afresh how young and unsophisticated Alexia looked.

"I am so . . . sorry to . . . intrude," she said in her soft, rather hesitating voice.

"It is no intrusion," the Marquis replied. "I am delighted to see you. I trust things are as satisfactory as you hoped they would be?"

Alexia did not reply and after a moment he said:

"I imagine, as you have come here, that you have something to tell me."

"I . . . I want your . . . help."

"Again?" the Marquis asked with a twist to his lips.

He saw that she was very nervous, and indicated, as he had done before, the chair facing the light.

She sat down in it and he remembered the way she held her back straight and put her hands together in her lap.

He noted, because he had an eye for detail, that the gown she was wearing was very simple and he suspected she had made it herself.

He fancied, being an expert on women's clothes,

that her face was framed by the same bonnet she had worn before, but the ribbons had been changed.

As Alexia did not speak he said in a gentler tone than he would have used to any other woman:

"I am waiting."

"I ... do not know where to ... begin."

The Marquis smiled.

"Then start at the beginning."

"Y-you have been ... so kind, so very kind ... and I am very, very grateful."

"That is what you said when you last left me."

"It is true," she said, "and that is why it seems so ... tiresome and unnecessary to ... trouble you again."

"But you are here, so it must be something important."

"It is ... to me."

"What is?" the Marquis asked.

She looked at him and he thought that her large grey eyes were more expressive even than her words.

Something was frightening her, something was perturbing her to the point where she had to have his assistance.

"Tell me about it, Alexia," he said.

"C-could you ... would you ... ask ... S-Sir Mortimer Walgrave to ... leave me alone?"

"Sir Mortimer Walgrave?"

It took the Marquis a second or two before he remembered a rather flashy middle-aged man who had often seemed unpleasantly noisy on race-courses.

The Marquis could not recall ever seeing him at any private functions and had certainly never made his acquaintance.

"What has Sir Mortimer to do with you?" he asked.

"I ... I have tried to send him away ... but he will not ... go. He calls all the time, and I know you will think it ... foolish ... but I am ... frightened of him!"

The Marquis knew when a woman was speaking

sincerely, and he could see too in Alexia's eyes exactly what she was feeling.

"How have you made this man's acquaintance, and what is your Chaperon, Mrs. Featherstone, doing about it?"

To his surprise, Alexia did not answer, but looked away from him in a manner which told him she was shy.

"Tell me," he ordered.

"It was ... Mrs. Featherstone who ... introduced us," Alexia said. "He is a ... f-friend of hers."

"Surely she realises he is not a suitable companion for you?"

"I think," Alexia said hesitatingly, "she ... does as he asks and ... and he brings her the sort of ... presents she wants."

"What sort of presents are those?"

Again Alexia looked uncomfortable and shy.

"Listen, Alexia," the Marquis said almost sharply, "if I am to help you you must tell me the truth—the whole truth."

"It seems so ... ungrateful ..." Alexia began to murmur, but the Marquis interposed:

"I asked you, what sort of presents?"

"M-mostly ... b-brandy."

"Are you telling me that Mrs. Featherstone drinks?"

He saw the answer in Alexia's face without her needing to reply.

"Good God!" he exclaimed. "I did not mean this sort of thing to happen."

He could see that Alexia was clutching her fingers together so tightly that the knuckles showed white.

"It is not only where I am c-concerned ... that it is very ... difficult," she said.

The Marquis waited, almost knowing what she was going to say.

"But he brings other ... men to the house ... the sort of gentlemen I ... do not want L-Letty to know,

and of whom, I am sure, Mama would not have . . .
approved."

The Marquis did not speak and after a moment
she went on, still in that hesitating, frightened little
voice:

"Th-they eat and drink so . . . m-much and we
really . . . cannot afford it."

"Have you not been to any Balls, Receptions, or
Assemblies?" the Marquis asked.

"Letty has been to one or . . . two Balls," Alexia replied, "but I do not think they were very . . .
grand ones."

"Why did you not accompany her?"

There was a little pause before Alexia answered:

"There was really not enough . . . money for me
to have . . . evening-gowns, and L-Letty looked so
beautiful that I felt it was a p-pity that the right sort
of . . . people were not . . . seeing her."

She looked at the Marquis pleadingly, as if she
begged him to understand.

He was frowning and after a moment she said:

"I have m-made you . . . angry. I did not . . .
wish to tell you these things . . . and I . . . I think I
could have managed somehow . . . if it had not been
for . . . Sir Mortimer."

"I am not angry with you," the Marquis said.

He did in fact feel extremely incensed at the idea
of a dissolute bounder like Mortimer Walgrave coming in contact with anything so sensitive and helpless
as Alexia.

"I am . . . so sorry to be . . . such a nuisance,"
she said, "but there was nobody else whose advice I
could ask . . . or who I could . . . turn to, and . . ."

She drew a deep breath before she added:

"Our . . . money has nearly all . . . g-gone!"

"In three weeks?" the Marquis ejaculated.

He knew without Alexia having to tell him exactly what had happened.

Mrs. Featherstone, relation or no relation, had
not proved the ideal Chaperon he had envisaged.

Being, as he had thought her, a pushing and importunate woman, she had turned the arrangement made by Mr. Dugdale to her own advantage.

Instead of doing her best for the two country girls, she had merely entertained at their expense.

If someone like Mortimer Walgrave took a fancy to one of her protégées, so long as he paid his way with brandy, then she was not going to interfere.

The Marquis, like most born organisers, which indeed he was, disliked almost fanatically his plans going awry.

If he set himslef out to achieve a certain objective, then nothing annoyed him more than that obstacles or difficulties should appear, especially if they were due to incompetence.

He told himself now the whole fault lay in the fact that neither he nor Dugdale had taken enough trouble to find out more about Mrs. Featherstone before installing her in the position of Chaperon.

They had just assumed that because she was a Minton before she married, because she had continually importuned the Marquis with letters asking for favours, that she was exactly the type of person they required.

For once the Marquis was not prepared to blame anybody but himself.

That Alexia was so vulnerable and so obviously helpless to deal with such a situation made him decide that something must be done and done immediately.

"P-please ... please forgive me," she was saying.

It flashed through his mind that there were few women who would not blame him in any way for what had occurred and only be humbly apologetic at being forced to worry him with her troubles.

Heaven knew he had had enough of other people's troubles thrust upon him in his life.

There had never been a love-affair when he had not found himself involved with a thousand problems that concerned the woman of his affections in one way or another.

Granted, the majority of them were financial, but there had been a great many other demons too, and to avoid being involved in them he had had to use a great deal of dexterity.

Alexia just sat looking at him with her enormous grey eyes, apologetic and at the same time worried in a manner which the Marquis found unexpectedly moving.

He rose to his feet to walk to the window, looking out unseeingly into the garden and wondering what the devil he could do about the whole tangle.

Then he remembered that his mother was upstairs.

"Wait here!" he said abruptly to Alexia, and walked out of the room, closing the door behind him.

He found his Comptroller in the Hall, looking a little agitated.

"I must apologise, My Lord," he said, "but I told the Butler you had an appointment in the Library —meaning that it was with me. He unfortunately misunderstood what I said and showed in Miss Minton as soon as she arrived."

The Marquis was still walking on as he listened to Mr. Dugdale's explanation.

"I should have seen her anyway, Dugdale," he said. "I will tell you about it later, but at the moment I have to speak to my mother."

He spoke in a tone which made his Comptroller look at him apprehensively, then went up the stairs two at a time and along the corridor to his mother's rooms.

She was sitting up in bed, having a cup of tea, when he entered.

There was a faint flush on her cheeks as if she had slept well, and the lines of tiredness had gone from her eyes.

"Chilton!" she exclaimed. "This is a lovely surprise!"

"I must have your advice, Mama."

"Of course!" his mother said. "Sit down. Would you like some tea?"

She indicated the tray laden with silver tea-things by her bed-side, but the Marquis shook his head.

"Do you remember a relation called Colonel Arthur Minton?" he enquired.

The Dowager Marchioness thought for a moment.

"Yes, I remember meeting him once a long time ago at somebody's wedding. He was very handsome, exceptionally so. I think he belongs to a distant branch of the family. Why do you ask?"

The Marquis sat down on the end of her bed as he used to do when a small boy and told her what had happened.

The Dowager Marchioness listened, with her eyes on his face, until he told her what he had just learnt from Alexia.

"I wish you had asked me," she said. "I could have told you a great deal about Sybil Featherstone, a most unpleasant woman, and certainly not the sort of person to be put in charge of two innocent young girls."

"How was I to know?" the Marquis asked.

"How could you, dearest? You would never have come in contact with such a creature, since she moves in a very different circle from yours. In fact it was your Aunt Emily who told me that she belongs to a very fast set."

"I should have found out about her before suggesting she should be put in charge of those two girls, who are nothing but children."

"It was kind of you to try and help them," the Dowager Marchioness said, "but it is a pity, if the younger one is as beautiful as you say, that they have wasted their money getting to know all the wrong people."

"That is what I feel," the Marquis agreed, "and as I feel rather responsible, I suppose I ought to do something to make amends."

His mother looked at him in surprise.

She had never known her son to put himself out in any way, and while she somewhat regretted what he frankly called his "selfishness" she had known there was nothing she could do about it.

"What I am asking you now, Mama," the Marquis said before she could speak, "is if you can give me the name of a suitable lady to look after these girls."

"Of course, dearest," the Dowager Marchioness said. "Why not me?"

Chapter Three

The Marquis came back into the Library and
Alexia saw at once that something had upset him.

He was looking crosser and more disagreeable
than he ever had before and she stared at him apprehensively as she rose nervously to her feet.

"My mother wishes to speak to you," he said,
and she thought his voice was harsh.

Because she could think of nothing to say she
merely followed him as he walked back the way he
had come, across the Hall and up the curved staircase.

If she had not been so troubled, Alexia would
have been thrilled with the magnificence of the house
and the pictures which they passed as they walked
down a wide corridor which led to the Dowager Marchioness's apartments.

The Marquis opened one door, then another, and
Alexia followed him into a bed-room.

"This is Alexia Minton, Mama," he said, and
she saw in a great canopied bed a very sweet face.

Alexia curtseyed, and in a gentle voice the Dowager Marchioness said:

"I am delighted to meet a Minton relative. My
son has been telling me about you and your beautiful
sister."

"His Lordship has been very kind to us," Alexia
managed to say.

She was acutely conscious that the Marquis was

Barbara Cartland

scowling as he walked across the room to stand in the sunshine of the big bow window.

"Come and sit down and tell me all about it," the Dowager Marchioness suggested.

As Alexia moved towards the bed she added:

"We must not keep you, Chilton. I am sure you have a mass of things to do."

"This is ridiculous, Mama, as I have already said," the Marquis answered. "I beg of you to consider before you raise Alexia's hopes."

"I have considered," the Dowager Marchioness replied, "and I know it will give me great pleasure to present such an attractive Minton to the Social World, while two of them makes it even more interesting."

Alexia started and looked at her wide-eyed.

"What I have been telling my son," said the Dowager Marchioness, "is that as you have been so unfortunate with Mrs. Featherstone, we must retrieve the situation, and I personally will chaperon you and your sister for the rest of the Season."

Alexia was speechless.

She was well aware of the Marquis's importance and she knew that if they were under his mother's wing every door in London would be opened.

"That is too ... marvellous to ... contemplate, Ma'am," she said, "but do not trouble about me. It is Letty of whom I am thinking."

"It is very unselfish of you, my dear," the Dowager Marchioness replied, "but you are the eldest and younger members of the family have to take their turn."

"That would be understandable in most families," Alexia said, "but Letty is so exceptionally beautiful, and I think His Lordship will have told you that that is why I was determined to bring her to London."

"I am looking forward to seeing your sister," the Dowager Marchioness said.

There was a pause, then Alexia murmured:

"I am afraid I could not . . . leave my little brother alone . . . even with Miss Graham to look after him."

"Your brother must of course be considered too," the Dowager Marchioness agreed.

"I am sure that . . . His Lordship will not . . . want him," Alexia said hesitatingly.

Alexia might have sensed, the Dowager Marchioness thought, because she was so perceptive, that the Marquis had already stormed:

"I will not have small children running all over my house, breaking things, putting sticky fingers on the tables, and making noise which I am sure will disturb you, Mama."

The Dowager Marchioness had smiled.

"You must have forgotten, Chilton, that the Nurseries are at the top of the house, and although you were an extremely noisy small boy you never disturbed me."

"What is your brother's name?" the Dowager Marchioness asked now.

"Peter, Ma'am."

"Then we must see that Peter is kept out of the way of my son, although I shall enjoy having a small boy round me again."

The Dowager Marchioness glanced at the Marquis's scowling face as she spoke and there was a faint twinkle in her eyes as she said:

"What I am going to suggest now is that while I get up, you go back to the house you have rented, pack up all your things, and return here with your family. Then, after we have had dinner you, I and Letty will plan our campaign."

She paused and, smiling, added:

"We are fortunate in that the Season will not end as early as it usually does, and I understand that the Prince Regent is to give a Fête towards the end of June."

Still the Marquis did not speak, and Alexia rose to her feet.

"I cannot begin to thank you, Ma'am, for your kindness," she said. "I am too overwhelmed to find the right words, and I can only say thank you from the bottom of my heart, as Letty will do when she hears about it."

It was obvious that her sincerity pleased the older woman and the Dowager Marchioness said:

"Well, run along, fetch Letty and Peter, and my son, who is so good at that sort of thing, will make arrangements for the carriages and of course to dispense with the services of Mrs. Featherstone."

"I suppose there is nothing I can do but obey you, Mama," the Marquis said, but he sounded far from pleased at the idea.

"You have always spoilt me, dearest Chilton," his mother remarked.

Alexia curtseyed and went from the room, followed by the Marquis.

They walked in silence for a little way down the corridor. Then when she was out of ear-shot of the Dowager Marchioness's apartments she stopped and looked up at him.

"Please ... My Lord," she said, "p-please ... listen to me for a ... moment."

"About what?" he asked ungraciously. "You have got your own way."

"I promise you ... I did not ... visualise that anything like this would ... happen," Alexia said, "and so ... although I am overwhelmed by your mother's kindness and generosity ... I think we had better go ... home."

The Marquis stared at her almost incredulously.

"I do not understand," he said. "Are you suggesting that you should refuse my mother's offer to chaperon you both?"

"I can see it would ... upset you," Alexia said, "and that would be ... wrong after you have been so kind to us. So it would be best if we went back to Bedfordshire and lived quietly as we were doing before I thought of ... coming to London."

She could not help a note of regret that was almost like a sob, but otherwise she spoke in a determined manner.

She was aware that the Marquis was staring at her searchingly and penetratingly, as if he questioned her sincerity and could hardly believe it possible.

"You are really saying," he said slowly after a moment, "that you will give up my mother's offer because you believe it will upset me?"

"I know you do not ... want us here," Alexia said. "When I came to you for help I did not ... mean to ask anything except that you should ... prevent Sir Mortimer Walgrave from ... frightening me."

"That is certainly something that neither he nor any of his kind will do in the future!" the Marquis exclaimed fiercely.

As he spoke he knew it had flashed through Alexia's mind that Sir Mortimer might, if she returned home, follow her to Bedfordshire.

Then as she lifted her chin a little the Marquis thought that he considered that that was immaterial.

Thinking he had accepted her suggestion, Alexia said:

"I would not wish to ... disturb your mother again ... so will you tell her how deeply grateful I am for her ... sympathy and understanding, and I shall always remember her in my ... prayers."

She started to walk once again down the corridor and after a moment's pause the Marquis followed her.

As they reached the top of the stairs he said in a different voice from the one he had used before:

"Having seen my mother, Alexia, you will understand that I love her and my greatest wish is to make her happy."

Alexia nodded her head, but she did not speak.

"She has set her heart on chaperoning you and your sister," the Marquis went on, "and has already decided you shall make your curtsey to the Queen."

Alexia, who had already descended some of the

49

stairs, now stopped and, holding on to the bannister with her hand, asked:

"Wh-what are you . . . saying? I . . . I am afraid I do not . . . understand."

"I am saying," the Marquis answered, "that I cannot allow my mother to be upset or thwarted. Therefore, we will do exactly as she has decided and you will fetch your sister and brother here as soon as you are packed."

Alexia stared at him, then said in a very low voice:

"You know I do not . . . wish to . . . upset you."

"I dare say I shall get used to the situation," the Marquis replied.

"Letty and I will not . . . intrude upon you in . . . any way," Alexia promised.

"Fortunately my house is a large one," the Marquis remarked, and they descended the rest of the stairs in silence.

After that Alexia felt as if she were in a dream.

The Marquis called for Mr. Dugdale and gave orders for a carriage to be brought round immediately.

In a few minutes Alexia found herself driving back the short distance to the house where they were staying in a comfort such as she had never imagined, with Mr. Dugdale beside her.

"Leave Mrs. Featherstone to me," he said. "Find your sister, and get a maid to pack your trunk."

"We have not a great deal to pack," Alexia answered. "Things are very expensive in London. I am afraid my estimates of what everything would cost were completely wrong."

Mr. Dugdale smiled.

"It is something I am always doing," he said, "underestimating, and finding the actual expenditure exceeds my limit."

He thought as he spoke that to spend more than was expected of His Lordship's money was very different from over-spending what this girl actually possessed.

"One thing," he said consolingly, "is that you no longer have to worry. Just leave everything to Her Ladyship. She is as clever an organiser as her son, although he would be annoyed to hear me say so."

"His Lordship ... does not ... want us," Alexia said in a low voice.

Mr. Dugdale smiled to himself.

"I think perhaps you might be very good for him," he said after a moment.

"Good for him?" Alexia queried.

"He is too young a man to get into a rut, to resent the unexpected and want everything to be tomorrow what it was yesterday."

Alexia thought this over for a moment. Then she said:

"He was angry at what his mother suggested, and I do not blame him. How could he possibly want not only Letty and me but also Peter in the house?"

"I doubt, when once you are installed, whether His Lordship will even realise you are there," Mr. Dugdale said. "The house is very large and when the old Marquis was alive there used to be a great many more poeple in it than there are at the moment."

"Was that due to the Marchioness?"

Mr. Dugdale nodded.

"Her Ladyship enjoys having people round her. She may say she dislikes being in London, but I have a feeling that it will give her back her youth, and the excitement of looking after you will make her look even more beautiful than she does at the moment."

"She is very ... very ... beautiful!" Alexia murmured.

She thought as she spoke that with the Dowager Marchioness and Letty she would certainly go unnoticed.

"I must look after Peter," she told herself, "and see that he does not interfere in any way with the Marquis."

When Letty heard the news of what was to happen, she was as speechless as Alexia had been, but her reaction was somewhat different.

"That means I shall see the Marquis again!" she exclaimed. "Oh, Alexia, I have thought about him so often since we came to London! I have never seen any gentleman who looks as smart or magnificent as he does."

Alexia had already told her sister that, while the Marquis was not at all pleased at the idea of his mother chaperoning them, he had accepted the situation rather than upset her.

"Do you think, as we will be staying with the Marquis, that we shall be invited to the Regent's Fête?" Letty asked.

"Perhaps . . . I do not know," Alexia replied. "I have heard very little about it."

"I have heard of nothing else!" Letty answered. "Two thousand people will be going, and Mrs. Featherstone is terrified that she will not get an invitation."

Thinking of Mrs. Featherstone made Alexia wonder uncomfortably what was happening downstairs.

She had on arrival at the house gone straight up to Letty's bed-room, where, as she had expected, her sister was lying down, having been very late getting home the night before.

Mrs. Featherstone had taken her to a party which from all accounts had been noisy and rather vulgar.

Letty had enjoyed it simply because everything was new and unexpected, although she had confessed to Alexia in the morning that several of the gentlemen who asked her to dance had been the worse for drink.

It was the sort of thing that Alexia dreaded happening, but it had been a relief to find that Letty had not taken their hiccupping compliments seriously.

She had also managed to avoid their flirtatious advances in a familiar manner, as if she were accustomed to doing so.

It was an inexpressible relief to know that she no

longer would have to lie awake worrying at night about
what sort of people Letty was meeting or whether she
would become involved with someone like Sir Mortimer Walgrave.

Although he had frightened Alexia with the things
he said to her and the way he always tried to get her
alone, she could only be thankful that it was not Letty
who had caught his fancy.

He was a horrible man and she had felt that he
encroached upon her menacingly.

Letty was so young, so beautiful, that as they
drove back to Osminton House Alexia could not help
feeling that when the Marquis saw her again his op-
position to their staying with him would crumble.

When they joined the Dowager Marchioness before dinner in what was known as the Small Salon,
Letty was looking her best.

Alexia had in fact dressed her herself in a gown
they had purchased since coming to London. It was
far prettier, besides being very much more expensive,
than anything Letty had ever worn before.

In white, trimmed with ribbons exactly the colour
of her thrush-egg-blue eyes, Letty looked like Per-
sephone heralding a new spring as she walked across
the Salon to curtsey extremely gracefully to the Dowager Marchioness.

"Alexia has told me, Ma'am, how kind you have
been to us," Letty exclaimed. "It is so terribly exciting! I keep thinking I must be dreaming and shall wake
to find myself at home in Bedfordshire, looking at the
flat countryside without even a tree to relieve the
monotony."

The Dowager Marchioness smiled.

"There are plenty of things in London to relieve
the monotony," she said. "I was told you were beautiful, and what was said about you was certainly not
exaggerated!"

"Thank you, Ma'am," Letty replied.

She did not blush or look surprised at the compliment, and Alexia realised she had had so many by

now that they had become quite a commonplace occurrence.

The Marquis entered the room and when Letty turned round to look at him she forgot about herself.

If he had seemed magnificent before, he was certainly overwhelmingly splendid in his evening-clothes.

His white cravat was tied in an intricate fashion which the girls did not realise was the despair of the Dandies who tried to emulate it and failed.

His jewellery consisted of only one magnificent and perfect black pearl in the centre of his evening-shirt.

His long-tailed coat fitted without a wrinkle, and although except for informal occasions the younger men of the *Beau Monde* wore tight-fitting trousers in the evening, the Marquis, because his mother preferred it, wore the satin knee-breeches and black silk stockings that had been obligatory in her day.

Letty stared at him for a moment, then she made a sound that was almost a cry of joy.

"How magnificent you are!" she exclaimed. "I am sure you should be the Regent. You would look so fine on the coins!"

She spoke with the spontaneous excitement of a child and her words swept away the faint shadow of a scowl that still remained between the Marquis's eyes.

"I am delighted to be appreciated by my guests," he said.

A little late, Letty remembered to curtesy.

"Alexia says you do not want us here, but I cannot tell you how thrilling it is for us, and we will be very, very good, I promise you."

Watching her son, the Dowager Marchioness said with a smile on her face:

"You cannot ask fairer than that, Chilton."

"No, indeed, Mama," the Marquis replied, kissing her hand, "and you know I am really concerned only with you."

"And with your own peace and quiet," the Dowager Marchioness added. "Well, we will do our best to oblige, as the servants say."

"That is something you always do for me," the Marquis answered.

"As you are in such a delightful mood," the Dowager Marchioness smiled, "perhaps I should just mention that tomorrow we are all going shopping."

At the word "shopping" Letty was suddenly alert, like a terrier, picking up her ears.

Alexia, however, gave her a quick frown which both the Dowager Marchioness and the Marquis noticed.

"That is very kind of you, Ma'am," she said, "but Letty and I have all we need."

She thought as she spoke that the Marquis looked disparagingly at the plain muslin evening-gown she wore, which she had made herself.

"Let me make one thing quite clear," the Dowager Marchioness said, "I do not intend to be deprived of what is the most exciting part of the London Season, and that is having better and more original gowns than anyone else."

She smiled at the Marquis as she said:

"You are too young to remember, dearest, but before the war I was always acclaimed as the best dressed in London. I could not bear now to be referred to as a 'has-been.' "

"You will never be that, Mama," the Marquis answered, knowing where the conversation was leading.

"As we shall all be appearing together," the Dowager Marchioness said, "we have to create a formidable front which none of our rivals will be able to challenge."

There was silence for a moment, then Alexia said:

"I am . . . afraid, Ma'am . . . that we . . ."

"I have changed my mind," the Dowager Marchioness interposed quickly. "Our gowns will be my contribution, while a Ball here at Osminton House will be my son's."

The Dowager Marchioness was still clinging to the Marquis's hand and now she looked up at him questioningly.

Just for a moment the Marquis hesitated: an emphatic refusal to entertain the idea hovered on his lips, then ruefully he replied:

"I suppose, Mama, the only thing left for me to do is to decide the date!"

"A Ball!"

The words burst from Letty's lips as if it was impossible for her to contain them.

"A Ball for Alexia and me! It is what Mama sometimes used to talk about, but I never thought it would ever be possible!"

Alexia's eyes were on the Marquis's face.

She felt he must be hating the idea and that they were imposing on him in a manner which made her feel ashamed. Yet there was nothing she could do about it.

As if he realised that she had not spoken, the Marquis turned to her.

"And what have you to say, Alexia?" he enquired.

"P-perhaps . . . if you really . . . hate the idea . . . Her Ladyship will . . . change . . . her mind," she stammered.

"I will do nothing of the sort!" the Dowager Marchioness retorted. "The Ball is not only for you, Alexia, and for Letty, it is also for me! It will be so marvellous to see the Ball-Room filled with my friends, and quite frankly, I have a great desire to wear the Osminton diamonds again before I have to pass them on to a daughter-in-law."

A daughter-in-law!

The words seemed to echo in Alexia's ears.

Mrs. Featherstone had been only too eager to list the number of conquests the Marquis had made amongst the great beauties of the *Beau Monde!*

She had also talked a great deal about Lady Harlow, but Alexia had understood that she was married.

Of course it was obvious that the Marquis, who was rich and important, would sooner or later take a wife.

Alexia could only hope humbly that if he did so it would not be before the Ball had been given at Osminton House at which the Social World could admire Letty.

As they sat down to dinner in the huge Dining-Room, where the walls were hung with the portraits of Minton ancestors and the Minton coat-of-arms was embroidered on the tapestry seats of the chairs, Alexia thought, like Letty, that it must all be a dream.

She had never imagined that a dining-table could look so beautiful decorated with gold candelabra, hot-house flowers, and Sèvres china.

As if he wished his mother to be happy and enjoy herself, the Marquis set himself out to be amusing.

He related stories of the Regent which made them laugh, he told of his successes in horse-racing and how he hoped to win the Gold Cup at Ascot.

More than once Alexia thought he looked at Letty as if he could hardly believe she was as beautiful as she appeared, with her eyes shining and her perfect cupid's-bow lips parted in her appreciation of everything she ate and saw.

Afterwards, when they withdrew with the Dowager Marchioness to the Salon, Alexia said:

"Would you excuse me, Ma'am, while I run upstairs and see if Peter is asleep?"

"But of course, dear," the Dowager Marchioness replied. "I am sure he is by now. He was so excited when he arrived."

"That is why I am afraid he may have found it difficult to sleep," Alexia said.

She was still feeling a little embarrassed by what had occurred when they had returned with Mr. Dugdale to Osminton House.

Peter had jumped up and down in the carriage in

a wild state of exhilaration because of the horses which were drawing it.

He loved horses, in fact it was a passion he had inherited from his father, and since he had been in London he had thought of nothing else.

Miss Graham had taken him to the Tower of London, where he had seen the tigers and lions, but, while he had talked about them for the next twenty-four hours, after that he had reverted to horses.

There had been no sign of the Marquis when the carriage drew up and Alexia had led the way upstairs, thinking that the sooner they all found their way to their own rooms the better.

She and Letty were to sleep near the Dowager Marchioness's Suite, while Miss Graham and Peter were to climb a floor higher to the old Nurseries.

The Housekeeper showed Letty her room, and Alexia, finding that hers was next door, was about to go upstairs to the Nurseries when she heard Miss Graham calling Peter.

"What is the matter?" Alexia asked.

Miss Graham put her head over the bannister.

"Is Peter with you, Alexia?"

"No," she replied. "I thought he was upstairs with you."

"He disappeared while I was attending to the luggage," Miss Graham said. "See if you can find him."

"I will."

Alexia hurried along the corridor, thinking that perhaps Peter had gone back to the Hall to have a last look at the horses which had drawn their carriage.

Then as she reached the top of the staircase she saw the Marquis come out of the Library, and she also saw her small brother.

He was standing there, staring up at the horses in the pictures painted by Stubbs.

Alexia was just about to call out to him when the Marquis, below her, said:

"You must be Peter!"

"Look at those horses!" Peter said, not even

turning his head in the Marquis's direction. "Just look at them! I want horses like those, but I want them real, not on the wall."

"Perhaps that is what you will have one day," the Marquis remarked.

It seemed to Alexia, watching, that Peter with difficulty took his eyes from the pictures to look up at the man standing beside him.

"Are the horses which brought us here yours?"

"They are," the Marquis answered.

"They are very fine!" Peter said. "Finer than any I have seen in the Park. Can I ride one of them?"

Alexia drew in her breath.

She wondered why she had not warned Peter that he must not ask such favours. She had meant to keep him away from the Marquis, who she was certain disliked small boys.

"Can you ride?" the Marquis enquired.

"Of course I can ride!" Peter replied. "I can jump too!"

"If we go to the country perhaps we could find you a pony."

"I do not want a pony," Peter said firmly, "I want horses like those."

He pointed at a Stubbs picture as he said:

"A big horse, and one that is spirited."

The Marquis laughed and put his hand on the boy's head.

"I am sure you will be getting into trouble if you do not go and find your sister," he said, and walked away, leaving Peter still staring up at the pictures.

Frightened in case he had made a bad impression on his host, Alexia called:

"Peter! Come upstairs at once!"

Because he was usually a good little boy Peter obeyed, and when he reached her she said:

"Surely you know you should have bowed to the Marquis and thanked him for having us here?"

"I was thinking about the horses," Peter said simply. "How many horses has he got?"

"I have no idea," Alexia answered. "And do understand, Peter, you are to stay upstairs in the Nurseries with Miss Graham, and you are never to come down to this part of the house alone."

Even as she spoke she knew that Peter was not listening. He had talked of nothing but horses all the evening, and she was certain now that he would either be thinking or dreaming about them.

She climbed up the stairs to the Nursery floor and found, as she had expected, that he was still awake.

He held out his arms to her and she sat down on the bed to hold him close against her.

"I have been thinking, Alexia," he said, "that the Marquis will keep his horses in his stables, and to-morrow I will go and see them."

"I will find out from Mr. Dugdale if that will be possible," Alexia replied, "but you must promise me, Peter, that you will not worry the Marquis about his horses or ask if you may ride them. We are so lucky to be here that we must do nothing to upset him."

"He said he would find me a pony," Peter said, "but I want a horse—a big horse. You know I can ride, Alexia."

It was true that Peter had ridden his father's horses because there had been nothing else available.

He had in fact loved horses ever since he had been able to walk.

Because Colonel Minton understood that what he felt himself was echoed in his son, he encouraged Peter from a very early age to ride in the front of his saddle and later to sit astride his own horse, looking absurdly small as he did so.

Where horses were concerned Peter was completely fearless. He fell off and got on again and seemed to have a way with horses that made old Joe, their father's groom, who was usually surly and disagreeable, permit him to do what he liked about the stable-yard.

But that was a very different thing, Alexia

thought, from making a nuisance of himself in the Marquis's stables.

She decided she would speak to Miss Graham in the morning and tell her how important it was that Peter should not be allowed out of her sight.

However, she knew it was no use sermonising now, as Peter would not listen, so instead she heard his prayers, kissed him affectionately, and left the door open in case he should be frightened in a strange house.

She was halfway down the staircase when the Marquis, coming from the Dining-Room towards the Salon, saw her.

Because she felt shy, as he looked up, Alexia's hands went instinctively to her hair, which she felt might have become untidy when Peter put his arms round her neck.

As she reached the Marquis she felt he was waiting for her to explain why she was not with his mother.

"I have been to say good-night to Peter," she said. "I am very sorry he was not more polite when he met you today, but he can think of nothing but horses."

"So I gathered!" the Marquis replied.

He spoke in a dry tone which did not tell Alexia anything, and because she could think of nothing else to say she moved ahead of him into the Salon.

They did not stay there long, as the Dowager Marchioness said she was tired and there was a great deal to do tomorrow.

"I will say good-night, dearest Chilton," she said. "And thank you for being so kind to me. I cannot tell you how happy I am to be here and to feel I can be of some use to our delightful cousins."

"It is wonderful to think you really are a relation," Letty enthused. "In fact, so that everybody shall know of it I think I shall walk about with a placard round my neck saying: *'I am a cousin of the Marquis of Osminton'!"*

The Marquis laughed.

"You might find that more of a disadvantage than an asset."

"Now you are being modest," Letty scoffed, "but thank you for being the most wonderful, kind, and generous cousin anyone could have."

She curtseyed as she spoke, and the Marquis bowed, but his eyes were twinkling.

Watching them Alexia wished that she could express half so eloquently what she felt filling her heart to overflowing.

Instead she could only curtsey, look up at the Marquis, and vainly try to find words.

"You are no longer worried, Alexia, I hope," the Marquis said, and she thought there was a cynical note in his question.

"There is ... nothing I can s-say except ... thank you!" she replied in a low voice.

She curtseyed to him very low and hurried after Letty.

They helped the Dowager Marchioness up the stairs and took her to her door, and she kissed them both good-night.

"Tomorrow we are really going to enjoy ourselves!" she declared. "There is nothing more fun than being really outrageously extravagant."

She smiled at them and when Letty reached her bed-room with Alexia, she flung herself on the bed, regardless of the damage it might do to her gown.

"Think of having new clothes, Alexia!" she cried. "Think of a Ball here in this enormous house and think of all the really exciting people we will meet!"

"The Marquis does not really wish to give a Ball," Alexia said in a low voice.

"But his mother intends to have one," Letty replied.

"I do not want him to feel that we are ... greedy and grasping," Alexia said, almost as if she spoke to herself.

"We are not!" Letty said positively. "And nothing is more infuriating than people who will not take what is offered them. Like servants who refuse a tip simply because they are too superior to accept one."

"When has that happened to you?" Alexia asked, diverted from her thoughts of the Marquis.

"Oh, somewhere Mrs. Featherstone took me," Letty replied casually. "It was a gaudy place where people bought drinks and coffee. The women who waited on us did not look like the usual waitresses and had their faces painted. Mrs. Featherstone said I was to pay the bill—as you know she never had any money with her—and the waitress refused most disdainfully."

Alexia said nothing and after a moment Letty went on:

"Mrs. Featherstone was angry. I think she was expecting to meet a gentleman, but he did not turn up."

Alexia drew in her breath.

She was quite sure from Letty's description that it was not at all the sort of place she should have gone to as a débutante.

Now that was all over, thanks to the Marquis and his mother, and she need not worry any more about her sister.

Later, when she had undressed, she knelt at the side of her bed and thanked God in the words she had been unable to say to the Marquis.

She thought as she prayed that it must have been her father and mother helping them, especially her mother.

"You always wanted us, Mama, to see a house like this," Alexia said, feeling sure in her heart that her mother could hear her, "and now Letty will have a chance of meeting the right type of people."

She paused before she added:

"And please, Mama, help us not to make any mistakes and antagonise the Marquis. I know he does not want us here, and you would have disapproved of our forcing ourselves upon him. And yet it is so wonderful for Letty!"

She waited, almost expecting to hear her mother's voice telling her that she had done the right thing. Then in the darkness a warm feeling of happiness enveloped her.

Alexia crept into bed.

It was a long time before she fell asleep.

*　　*　　*

The next three days were spent in shopping.

Alexia had never thought for a moment, had never imagined, how tiring it would be to stand trying on beautiful gowns, choosing attractive bonnets, shoes, gloves, reticules, and sun-shades.

There were also the most exquisite underclothes that were so fine and transparent that she found herself blushing when she wore them.

She had meant to persuade the Dowager Marchioness to concentrate entirely on Letty and had actually planned that the gowns they had bought for Letty previously could be altered for her.

But the Dowager Marchioness had been very firm.

"I am presenting you both to the Social World," she said, "and I intend to be very proud, Alexia, not only of your sister but also of you!"

"Nobody will notice me with you and Letty there, Ma'am," Alexia replied.

The Dowager Marchioness gave her one of her sweet smiles.

"You are making the foolish mistake, my dear, of comparing people to the glorification of one and the detriment of another. Everyone is different, everyone has been created in a different image which is peculiarly their own."

She saw that Alexia was listening intently and went on:

"If you asked me which is the most beautiful, a rose, an orchid, or a lily, I would be unable to answer you, and the same applies to people. You, Alexia, are as beautiful in your own way as Letty is in hers."

"I have never . . . thought of myself as . . . beautiful," Alexia protested, "but my eyes are like . . . Mama's."

"I remember people telling me that she was very lovely," the Dowager Marchioness said quietly.

Alexia looked at herself that evening wearing a new evening-gown which the Dowager Marchioness had given her.

It was in the very latest fashion and she thought that perhaps she did look quite pretty, and that now the Marquis would not be ashamed of her.

She was sure he had noticed last night how plain her gown was and she could understand now what he must have thought. The gown she was now wearing revealed the perfection of her figure and seemed a frame for her white skin.

Letty looked absolutely radiant, and her hair, dressed in the latest mode, seemed to hold the sun, which had been shining all day.

It was not really a surprise but what might have been expected, Alexia thought, when after they had dined the Dowager Marchioness said:

"I am now taking you to a small Reception at Richmond House. The Duchess is anxious to meet you both and it will be nice for you to make some new friends before we appear at one of the great Balls which will be taking place next week."

They had dined alone, as the Marquis, Alexia learnt, was at Carlton House.

She could not help hoping that he would see Letty looking so beautiful and his mother hinted that he might join them later in the evening.

Richmond House was almost as grand as the Marquis's, although the pictures were undoubtedly not so exceptional.

There was however a party of about fifty people, and Alexia knew with pride that Letty created a sensation the moment she entered the room.

Not only did the gentlemen cluster round her but the women talked about her in almost awe-struck tones,

while the Dowager Marchioness was welcomed effu-
sively by many of her old friends.

"It is wonderful to see you!" they said over and
over again. "I thought you never came to London."

"If I cannot stay too late at the Balls I shall rely
on someone to look after these dear girls, and if I want
a night in bed I shall be very disappointed if I do not
find a friend who will take my place," the Dowager
Marchioness replied.

There was a chorus of offers to assist her and
Alexia felt that the anxiety about Letty that had kept
her tense and perpetually worried was swept away.

Now everything was going to be all right. Now
everything would be exactly as she wanted it to be!

There were a number of older men whom the
Dowager Marchioness presented to her and they told
her things about the political situation which she found
absorbingly interesting.

She was in fact talking to a Member of Parliament called William Wilberforce, who was campaign-
ing for reform, when she looked up to see that the
Marquis had arrived.

She thought it was because he looked so impressive and seemed to tower over every other man in the
room that her heart gave a leap at the sight of him.

Having kissed his hostess's hand he went to his
mother's side and she smiled at him, obviously over-
joyed that he had kept his promise.

"You are not too tired, Mama?" the Marquis
asked.

"To tell you the honest truth, Chilton, I feel as if
I am floating on a cloud! Perhaps it is the champagne
or perhaps it is because it is so warming to be back
amongst my old friends, who have welcomed me so
kindly."

"I told you not to stay so long in the country,"
the Marquis said.

"And you were right, dearest, as you always are.
Tell me, what do you think of your cousins?"

The Marquis looked to where Letty was being

paid fulsome compliments by some gentleman he
recognised as being usually too blasé to speak to girls.

His eyes were twinkling as he looked towards
Alexia.

Because she thought she was being rude in watching him, her face was now raised towards Mr. Wilberforce's as he explained how he was supporting a Bill
which would abolish the use of "Climbing Boys" to
clean chimneys.

Alexia's expression was serious and it was obvious from her eyes that she was deeply in sympathy
with everything Mr. Wilberforce was telling her.

The Marquis looked at her for some seconds. Then
he said:

"I think, Mama, it is time I took you home."

"It will take me a little time to say good-night to
all my friends," the Dowager Marchioness replied,
"but I will start at once."

It was indeed nearly twenty minutes before they
finally walked downstairs, the charming things their
hostess and other members of the party had said still
ringing in their ears.

"They were really glad to see me," the Dowager
Marchioness said happily.

"That is not surprising," the Marquis replied.

"And you, my dears," she said to Alexia and Letty, "were the sensations I wanted you to be."

"I feel exactly like a butterfly that has just burst
out of its chrysalis!" Letty said. "I had no idea I had
such beautiful wings."

The Dowager Marchioness laughed.

"And you, Alexia? What did you find?"

"I found Mr. Wilberforce extremely interesting,"
Alexia replied. "I do hope ... everyone will ... support the Bill to abolish Climbing Boys."

She looked anxiously at the Marquis as she spoke,
feeling that if he said he would not do so it would be
like a blow.

"I have already promised my support," he said,
and saw her eyes light up with pleasure.

"He is also against . . . slavery," she murmured.

"You take everything far too seriously," he remarked as they reached the Hall and his mother was being helped into her fur-trimmed wrap.

"Too seriously?" Alexia questioned.

"You are here to enjoy yourself, not to worry over suffering humanity or anything else."

"But it is so important!" Alexia replied. "And surely these terrible cruelties and injustices should concern everyone?"

The Marquis did not answer.

He wondered when he had last heard a woman of his acquaintance show the slightest concern over the crusades to which a few Evangelistic men had dedicated themselves.

Chapter Four

The Marquis, driving his superb horses and high-perch Phaeton towards Chelsea, decided this was the last time he would have a love-affair with any woman in the Social World.

Ever since he had promised his mother that he would have no more to do with Imogen Harlow she had bombarded him with letters, at first commanding him to come to her, then pleading, and finally becoming abusive.

He began to think that perhaps his mother was right in imagining that somehow and by some devious means of her own Imogen had intended to inveigle him into marriage.

But her behaviour, since he had intimated that their association was at an end, had been so unpleasant that it had given him a distaste for any further *affaires de coeur* of that kind.

"In the future," he swore to himself, "I will stick to doxies! They are no trouble. They keep their place and have no ambitions beyond emptying one's pockets."

It was expected that a gentleman who was a Corinthian and in the Georgian term a "Full Man" should keep a mistress.

Renée Duval was one of many who had come and gone from the attractive house that stood in Royal Avenue, Chelsea, near the Hospital founded by Nell Gwynne.

Renée was appearing at the Lyceum Theatre, which had been taken over for the Royal Drury Lane Company after their famous Theatre had been burnt down in 1809.

The blaze had lit all London and it had also ruined Richard Brinsley Sheridan, who owned it.

A lesser man would have collapsed, but characteristically he started all over again, with the help of Samual Whitbread, a brewer and a Member of Parliament.

It was expected that Drury Lane would reopen next year and in the meantime most of the original cast drew large audiences to the Lyceum.

The Marquis had noticed Renée the first time he had attended *The Country Girl*, a play in which originally Mrs. Jordan, mistress of the Duke of Clarence, had played the lead. In his usual imperious way he had swept aside all other contestants and carried Renée off in triumph.

She was in appearance the exact opposite of Imogen Harlow. Dark, with slanting eyes, she was not strictly beautiful but she had that fascination which in a Frenchwoman is more alluring and seductive than beauty itself.

She was full of *joie de vivre* and used every wile and sophisticated charm to amuse and captivate her protector.

As it happened, however, the Marquis had not called at number 6 Royal Avenue for some weeks.

He had been busy before his mother had arrived to stay, and since then, what with the Prince Regent, his mother, and his débutante cousins, he felt that he had not had a moment to himself.

But this evening, he had learnt, Renée was not appearing on the stage, as another play was to be introduced the following day in which she was to have the leading role.

"She will be resting," the Marquis told himself with a smile, "if I allow her to do so!"

His thoughts, however, wandered from the anticipation of what lay ahead to the sensation which Letty had caused last night.

It had in fact been the most important Ball of the Season, given by the Duchess of Melchester for her own débutante daughter and attended by everyone of importance in the *Beau Monde,* starting with the Prince Regent.

The Dowager Marchioness, with the skill of a professional stage-manager, had deliberately kept the dinner-party which they had given at Osminton House from arriving at the Ball too early.

She had in fact waited until all the Dowagers were seated on the dais from which they watched the dancers.

At the same time, the majority of the gentlemen were still making no effort to dance but were standing about, talking to one another and appraising the women as if they were at a horse-sale.

It was a night when the Dowager Marchioness knew that every woman would be wearing her best gown and every jewel she possessed.

The gentlemen were equally resplendent, wearing their decorations as the Prince Regent was to be present, and no-one could have looked more impressive than the Marquis himself.

The Dowager Marchioness glittered in the huge diamond tiara, almost like a crown, which had been in the Osminton family for a century.

There was a diamond necklace which was almost blinding in its brilliance, with bracelets, rings, and ear-rings of the same blue-white stones to complete the collection.

She knew that she would be noticed even among a large crowd, as she had been all her life, and she was determined that the two girls whom she was to chaperon should receive the same attention.

71

Letty, as was to be expected, wore white, but it was a white that was different from that worn by any of the other débutantes.

The white gauze of which the gown was made was decorated with white roses, each petal shimmering with a diamanté dew-drop.

Roses encircled the neck of her gown, and there was a wreath for her golden hair, with bracelets to match on her wrists above her short gloves.

The whole effect was, Alexia thought, quite breathtaking, and she knew that it would be impossible for Letty's beauty not to shine like a light even in a crowded Ball-Room.

She had not expected that she too would attract any attention, but the Dowager Marchioness had chosen her gown also with care.

It was of silver gauze and made her look as if she were dressed in moonlight.

Round her neck she wore a very simple necklace of turquoises, which only the Dowager Marchioness had been clever enough to realise were the stones which best accentuated Alexia's spiritual beauty and gave prominence to her large grey eyes.

Instead of a wreath there were two brooches of turqouises and diamonds to wear in her soft, fair hair.

As Alexia looked at herself in the mirror she wished above all else that her mother could see her. Then she told herself that she was sure she could do so and that she was pleased.

'This is how you would want Letty and me to look, Mama,' she said in her heart. 'How can we ever be grateful enough for the kindness we have received from the Marquis and his mother?'

While the older women at the dance congratulated the Dowager Marchioness on the girls' appearance, the men bombarded the Marquis to introduce them.

He told himself wryly that it was certainly something new for him to be introducing women who ostensibly belonged to him to aspiring swains.

He found it, however, difficult to remain cynical and aloof when the Prince Regent said to him:

"I cannot imagine, Chilton, why you always get the best of everything! I should hardly have imagined that young girls were much in your line, and yet you manage to produce superlative examples who outclass every other one in the room!"

"I have enjoyed myself!" the Dowager Marchioness said as they drove home.

"It was wonderful! Wonderful!" Letty cried. "I never dreamt I could have such a glorious time, or have so many partners that I had to divide my dances into two."

"You were the success I had hoped for," the Dowager Marchioness said simply.

She smiled at Letty, then put her hand on Alexia's, who was sitting beside her.

"And you were a success too, my dear," she said softly. "Several men told me that they not only found you beautiful but very intelligent."

Alexia blushed.

"It was such a . . . splendid gathering," she said in her soft voice, "something I shall . . . remember all my life."

The Marquis drove them to Osminton House.

"You are not coming in?" his mother asked as he said good-night on the door-step.

"No, Mama, I have done my duty and I think I am entitled to my time off."

"You certainly are!" the Dowager Marchioness replied. "And we are grateful to you for looking after us all so well."

"Yes, indeed!" Letty interposed enthusiastically. "Everybody was terribly impressed that we are your cousins and are actually staying at Osminton House!"

The Marquis laughed, but as Alexia heard the carriage drive away she longed to ask where he was going.

The stories which Mrs. Featherstone had told her

of his many lady-friends came crowding back into her mind, and she wondered if he thought them more beautiful than Letty, while undoubtedly they would be more entertaining.

"Anyone he . . . loved would have to be very . . . very exceptional," she told herself, and wondered why the idea was so depressing.

*   *   *

The Marquis drew his horses up outside number 6 Royal Avenue and gave the reins to his groom.

"Walk the horses, Jason," he said. "I do not suppose I shall be here for more than an hour."

He then remembered that he had not announced his coming, and added:

"Wait until you see me enter the house. The lady on whom I am calling may not be at home."

It occurred to him for the first time that he had been slightly highhanded to expect his mistress to be waiting for him when he had not bothered to communicate with her for nearly a month.

Then he told himself that as long as he paid the rent and the expenses of the house, and gave her a number of presents, she was hardly in a position to complain.

He knocked loudly on the door, but it was some minutes before it was opened by a maid, who was also in his employment.

"Is *Mademoiselle* at home?" he enquired.

"Yes, M'Lord, but she didn't tell me she was expecting Your Lordship."

"She does not know," the Marquis replied.

He handed the maid his hat and as he did so she said:

"*M'mselle*'s been washing her hair, but you'll find her M'Lord, in the Drawing-Room."

The Marquis went up the stairs without hurrying and opened the Drawing-Room door.

Renée was lying on the couch, her dark hair, which was one of her most attractive features, falling over the shoulders of her transparent negligee. There was a box of chocolates by her side.

She looked up from the script she was reading, saw the Marquis, and gave a cry that was undoubtedly one of delight.

"Milor! Je pense you forget me!"

She would have risen to her feet but the Marquis crossed the room before she could do so and sat down on the side of the couch, facing her.

"You look very alluring like that," he said, pulling her negligee from her shoulders, "and it certainly saves time."

"I am angry *contre toi*," Renée pouted as she said in her fascinating French accent. "You neglect me for so very long and do not ask me to pardon you."

"But you will do so," the Marquis said, "because I have brought you a present."

"A present?"

Her eyes, which had been reproachful, lit up and she put out her hands.

The Marquis drew from his pocket the bracelet which he had bought for Imogen Harlow and then decided not to give to her.

It was very expensive and it seemed a pity to waste it.

He put the leather box into Renée's hands. She opened it and gave an exclamation which was both one of astonishment and one of delight.

"You're so very . . . very kind, *Milor!*" she said. *"Alors,* I forgive you for making me *tres triste."*

The Marquis took the bracelet from the box and clasped it round her wrist.

"C'est magnifique!" Renée exclaimed.

"And now you must pay for it," the Marquis answered, and pulled her into his arms.

*   *   *

Driving back to Osminton House, not an hour later as he had intended but after the clock on Chelsea

Hospital had struck midnight, the Marquis thought he had been right.

In the future he would have nothing more to do with married women, whose husbands, complaisant or otherwise, always constituted a danger.

He was also tired, he told himself, of entering a house quietly after the servants had retired for the night and leaving surreptitiously in case he should be seen by some acquaintance who might be passing by.

He was bored with being involved in love-affairs which ended with the woman reproachful, in tears, and full of recriminations.

Renée was, he told himself, very satisfactory in the part which she was expected to play where he was concerned.

Granted, her conversation was somewhat limited, but he usually never stayed long enough to find it necessary to have one.

Tonight, because he had not been with her for so long, he had given in to her pleadings that he should dine with her, and had enjoyed an extremely well-cooked meal of French dishes.

He drank with them some excellent wines which had been taken to the house from his own cellars and which were served at exactly the right temperature.

"One thing about Frenchwomen," he told himself, "is that they know as much about food as they do about love-making."

They had dined late and Renée had thanked him profusely for the second time for his present, which had necessitated his seeing her again with her dark hair falling over her bare shoulders.

"Milor! Come very soon?" she questioned when he left her.

"You will certainly be busy for the next few days with this new play," the Marquis replied.

"Toujours, there is the afternoon," she replied. "I not accept the many invitations I have to supper if I eat with you."

"I will let you know when I am free," the Marquis promised.

Then he had gone out into the warm night air, feeling satisfied and at peace with the world.

As he drove back to Park Lane, however, his thoughts were not on Renée, as might have been expected.

Instead, he was considering whether he should buy two horses which he had heard earlier in the day were for sale since their owner needed ready money to pay his gaming debts.

The Marquis's knowledge of horse-flesh was renowned throughout the racing world, and he was determined both to win the Gold Cup at Ascot next week and also several other races at the same meeting.

He was spending not only a lot of his money but a great deal of his time in breeding fine horses and having them trained by a man he considered to be the best trainer in the country.

At the same time, he was the first to admit that there was always room for improvement, and he thought that these two horses would add considerably to his breeding stock. He wanted soon to lead in the winner of the Grand National.

As he drew up outside his own house, he was thinking with a smile on his lips what a triumph this would be.

"Thank you, Jason," he said to his groom as he stepped down and walked into the Hall.

To his surprise he found a number of people gathered there.

In the centre of them he saw Alexia, and talking to her was his Comptroller, wearing a long robe over his night-shirt. He had obviously been awoken after going to bed.

There was an elderly woman wearing a flannel dressing-gown who he imagined must be Miss Graham, several footmen, and besides them two night-watchmen.

One of the footmen hurried to take the Marquis's hat and as everyone else turned to look at him he asked:

"What is going on? Why are you all here?"

He addressed Alexia and he saw by the expression on her face that something untoward had happened.

"Peter is missing," she replied.

Then, as if she was afraid that the information would make the Marquis angry, she added:

"I am so sorry . . . I cannot imagine what has occurred . . . but he is not in his room . . . and we have looked . . . everywhere in the house . . . but we cannot find him."

"Does my mother know of this?" the Marquis asked.

"No, no! Of course not! We have not disturbed her," Alexia answered quickly. "We came back from the Ball and it was after Her Ladyship and Letty had gone to bed that Miss Graham told me that Peter's bed was empty."

"I do not know what made me go into his bedroom, My Lord," Miss Graham interposed, "but I woke up feeling anxious for no good reason, and went to see if he was all right, but he was not in his bed."

"A footman fetched me, My Lord," Mr. Dugdale added, "and I have had the whole house searched, but there is not a sign of him. I cannot imagine what has happened."

"I am . . . sorry to worry you," Alexia said, "but we must find him . . . and I cannot think why he should . . . hide himself."

There was something desperate in her tone which made the Marquis answer with an almost exaggerated calm:

"I am sure he cannot have gone far, and I can hardly imagine that he would be kidnapped from this house."

"No-one has passed through this door, M'Lord!" one of the footmen exclaimed.

"And he couldn't have gone out of th' kitchen door without us seeing him, M'Lord," a night-watchman cried.

The Marquis thought for a moment.

That meant that the only way Peter could have left the house would be through one of the windows into the garden.

As if she knew what he was thinking Alexia said quickly:

"The footmen have searched the garden. I thought perhaps he might have gone to feed the goldfish. He feeds them every morning."

The Marquis realised that everyone in the Hall was looking at him, waiting for him to find a solution to the problem.

He thought that in Alexia's eyes and indeed in some of the others' there was an expression of trust which he had seen in the eyes of his spaniels, who were always at his heels when he was in the country.

"I suppose no-one has thought of the stables?" he said at length.

"Of course!" Alexia cried. "That is where he will have gone! Why did I not think of it?"

"That is where you and I will go at once," the Marquis said.

He turned to his Comptroller.

"That will give you, Dugdale, time to dress in case we have to look further afield, and also order some soup or a warm drink for the boy when we bring him back."

The Marquis did not wait for an answer but walked across the Hall and into the Library. Alexia followed him.

The curtains were drawn and the Marquis pulled one back and unlatched the long French window which led out into the garden.

"Peter obviously did not leave the house this way," he said, "but there are a number of windows he could have opened."

"I forgot that the nearest way to the stables was through the garden," Alexia said.

"I have lived here longer than you have," the Marquis answered, "and I gather from the short acquaintance I have had with Peter that his one interest is horses."

"It is an obsession!" Alexia cried. "I believe he goes to the stables whenever Miss Graham will take him there."

She was feeling as she moved with the Marquis over the soft grass that if anything happened to Peter it would be her fault.

She had been so busy with Letty, shopping with her, and attending, with the Dowager Marchioness, Receptions, Assemblies, and musical evenings, besides driving in the Park, that she felt now her small brother had been neglected.

'Miss Graham is getting too old for him,' she thought, 'and he needs a Tutor.'

Then she remembered guiltily that when they had been at home she had herself given him some lessons every day.

"Are you blaming yourself?" the Marquis asked with a dry note in his voice, which always made her feel apologetic.

"H-how . . . did you know?" she questioned.

"I felt it would be your natural reaction," he replied. "You try to carry all the burdens of the world upon your shoulders, Alexia, and I assure you it is quite unnecessary to do anything of the sort."

"B-but if I do not . . . look after Peter myself . . . you see what happens!" Alexia replied. "It was wrong of me not to spend more time with him . . . and very . . . s-selfish."

"I think that like most women you like to think yourself indispensable," the Marquis remarked, and Alexia knew it was not a compliment.

She longed to reply that she was indispensable to Peter simply because they could not afford the Tutor whom a wealthy child would have at his age. Miss Graham was too old and too slow for him.

But it would have been impossible to ask the Marquis to extend his favours any further and she had no intention of doing so.

They reached the end of the garden, passing through great banks of rhododendrons, until in the wall which Alexia guessed bordered the Mews there was a door.

The Marquis opened it and she found herself facing his stables, which filled nearly the whole Mews running parallel to Park Lane.

The horses of the Phaeton in which the Marquis had returned from Chelsea were being taken from between the shafts, and when he appeared, an elderly man came through from one of the open stable doors.

"Good-evening, M'Lord!" he said. "Is anything wrong?"

"You know Master Peter, the young gentleman who is staying with me?" the Marquis asked. "He has apparently disappeared, Sam, from his bed-room, and I thought he might have come here."

"I've not seen 'im, M'Lord, not since this mornin'," Sam replied. " 'E fair dotes on them horses, an' I'd quite a tussle with him, I did, over Belladonna."

"Why was that?" the Marquis asked.

"Well, Sir, Master Peter naturally wanted to see 'er, M'Lord, seein' as 'ow she only arrived from the Sale-Room two days ago. But the animal ain't safe. I was intending to speak to Your Lordship about her."

"Not safe?" the Marquis queried.

"The stable-lads be frightened to go near 'er, M'Lord. I'm hopin' as 'ow 'er'll calm down in a day or two, but at th' moment she be in a nasty temper!"

He paused to say positively:

"I'd not let anyone into 'er stable—least of all Master Peter, M'Lord, however brave, 'e may be!"

"You are quite right," the Marquis said, "but suppose we start looking elsewhere?"

"O'course, M'Lord," Sam agreed hastily, and started to open the top part of each of the stable doors.

The horses had been bedded down for the night. Most of them were resting quietly and turned their heads almost resentfully as the lantern Sam held in his hand lit up the darkness.

They went from one stall to another but there was no sign of Peter in any of them, and as they approached the last one Sam said:

"I'm sorry, M'Lord, but it looks as though we've drawn a blank!"

There was one stall left and as Alexia walked towards it Sam said hastily:

"That's where I put Belladonna, Miss. She's quiet now, but she was kicking up a real hullabaloo earlier this evenin' and I'd rather you didn't disturb 'er."

"I understand . . ." the Marquis began to say, when Alexia gave a little dry.

"The door . . . it is not fastened!"

Sam gave an exclamation of astonishment and moved forward with his lantern.

It was true—the lower half of the door, which was usually secured by an iron bolt, was undone.

Hastily with fingers which shook with anxiety the old groom undid the top half of the door and held up the lantern.

The mare was asleep and beyond her in the corner of the stable was a small figure lying down.

Alexia felt as if everything swam before her eyes.

She could understand what had happened: Peter had entered the stall in his usual confident manner and the mare had either kicked or savaged him.

Now he was injured, perhaps dead!

Instinctively she put out her hand to hold on to the Marquis and felt his fingers close over hers.

She could not speak, she could not even think.

"Shall I fetch 'im out, M'Lord?" Sam asked in a low voice.

As he spoke, Belladonna turned her head and

put back her ears. She also drew back her lips from her teeth.

The Marquis did not answer. He was staring intently at Peter in the far corner of the stall. Then he said very softly:

"Call him, Alexia, not loudly but enough to waken him."

For a second Alexia looked up at him in astonishment, then obediently in a voice that quivered she said:

"Peter! Peter!"

She thought he must be dead, and she had no hope of arousing him. Then Peter moved, opened his eyes, and yawned.

"Peter!" she said again.

"I—must have—fallen asleep!" he said in a drowsy voice.

He sat up slowly and without haste rose to his feet.

As the three people watching him held their breath he moved towards the horse and put his arms round her neck.

"Good-night, Belladonna," he said. "I will come and talk to you again tomorrow."

He rested his cheek against her, then yawning once again walked towards the door.

Sam opened it for him, muttering as he did so:

"I've never seen nothin' like it—not in all me born days!"

Alexia was down on her knees on the cobblestones, holding Peter close against her.

"Oh, darling, you gave us all such a fright! How could you have done anything so naughty?" she asked. "How could you have come here in the middle of the night?"

"Belladonna was unhappy," Peter replied. "I heard her when I was in the garden, before I went to bed, but Miss Graham would not let me go to her."

He yawned again before he said:

"I knew she wanted me, and when I talked to her she was not unhappy any more."

It was impossible for Alexia to answer him because the tears were running down her cheeks. She could only hold him close, her lips against his hair.

"Belladonna will go to sleep now," Peter said to Sam.

The old groom was incapable of replying, and as Alexia rose a little unsteadily Peter said:

"I am tired. Carry me, Alexia, I am too tired to walk."

"I will carry you," the Marquis said.

He picked the small boy up in his arms and Peter put his arms round his neck.

"I love all your horses," he murmured sleepily, "but I think I love Belladonna the best!"

Sam had shut the door of the stall and stood looking at the Marquis as if he expected to be reprimanded.

"I think in order to prevent this sort of thing from happening a second time you had better take Master Peter riding every morning," the Marquis said. "I am sure you have a horse that will suit him."

"I would like to ride Hercules," Peter said.

"Then Hercules it shall be," the Marquis agreed. "Good-night, Sam!"

"Good-night, M'Lord," the groom replied.

There was still an expression of incredulity on his face and in his voice.

Alexia wiped away her tears and followed the Marquis back to the garden door.

As they walked across the garden she realised that Peter had fallen asleep, his head resting on the Marquis's shoulder, his forehead tucked in against his chin.

"Why did I not . . . guess that was . . . where Peter would be?" she asked as if she was speaking to herself.

"Because you have never been a small boy," the Marquis replied. "I played truant after I was supposed to be in bed in this house and very often at the Castle, and I have not forgotten it."

"He might have stayed there all night."

84

The Problems of Love

"Incredible though it seems, he would have come to no harm," the Marquis replied. "Has he always had this gift with horses?"

"He has loved those he has known," Alexia replied. "But he has never had a chance to do anything like this before."

"I look forward to seeing him ride."

"It is very ... kind of you ... but I think it is a ... mistake."

"A mistake?" the Marquis questioned.

She knew, although she could not see his face, that he had raised his eye-brows.

By this time they had reached the house, and when the Marquis went through the open Library window followed by Alexia, they found that Mr. Dugdale and Miss Graham were waiting for them.

Both had dressed hurriedly, and there was also the Butler, who had obviously just been aroused, standing in the background.

"You have found him!" Mr. Dugdale exclaimed in a tone which expressed his relief.

"We found him in the stall with that new mare I bought two days ago," the Marquis answered, "the one which has terrified the stable-boys and even old Sam himself!"

"He is unharmed?" Mr. Dugdale asked.

"Completely!" the Marquis smiled. "He put his arms round the mare and kissed her good-night! If I had not been there myself I should have refused to believe the story!"

"I am sorry this should have happened, M'Lord," Miss Graham said. "Shall I carry him upstairs?"

"I think I will take him up myself," the Marquis answered. "He is tired and who shall blame him? It is somewhat exhausting trying to calm a horse that is kicking down the stables!"

He spoke almost mockingly, and yet Alexia thought that he was pleased with Peter and it gave her a warm feeling in her heart.

But as Miss Graham hurriedly followed the Mar-

85

quis into the Hall and up the stairs, Alexia remained in the Library.

"I am sorry you have been upset, Miss Alexia," Mr. Dugdale said.

Alexia gave a sigh.

"I was frightened ... terribly frightened that something had happened to him," she said. "One hears such terrible stories of the things that can occur in London."

She was thinking of the Climbing Boys as she spoke, having learnt from Mr. Wilberforce that many of them were stolen when they were young and forced by the cruel Sweeps to go up chimneys that were still hot so that their feet and arms were burnt.

"Your brother is a very intelligent little boy, Miss Alexia," Mr. Dugdale said, "but you must tell him tomorrow that it is a mistake to be too adventurous and too inquisitive."

"I have told him often enough," Alexia replied, "but I very much doubt if he listens to me."

Mr. Dugdale smiled.

"As I have often found out, it is difficult to learn from someone else's mistakes," he said. "But try not to worry about him."

He hesitated, then he added:

"Perhaps at his age it would be a good idea for him to have a Tutor. If you will not think it impertinent of me or that I am interfering, I think he needs more advanced lessons than those Miss Graham can give him."

"I know that," Alexia replied. "I have known it for a long time, but we cannot afford to pay a Tutor."

"Suppose I speak to His ..." Mr. Dugdale began.

"No, no! Certainly not!" Alexia interrupted. "His Lordship has done so much for us already and we are so deeply in his debt that ... I ... I want to speak to him about it when he returns."

"I understand. Good-night, Miss Alexia, and I can only say that 'All's well that ends well.'"

The Problems of Love

"Thank you, Mr. Dugdale. I am sorry they got you out of bed."

"I was not asleep, as it happens, I was reading. It is the only time of the day I have the chance to keep up with my own interests."

He smiled at Alexia and left the room, and she moved about restlessly to stand finally looking at a portrait of the Marquis's mother which had been painted soon after she married.

She was so beautiful that it was impossible to think that any other Marchioness of Osminton could have equalled her.

It suddenly struck Alexia that a portrait of Letty wearing the Osminton diamonds might one day hang in the Picture Gallery amongst the family portraits.

She wondered why it had never occurred to her before that Letty might marry the Marquis, and she wondered too why the idea, instead of being one of elation, made her feel suddenly as if she carried a stone within her breast.

And was it such a far-fetched notion? She knew that the Dowager Marchioness was longing for the Marquis to marry.

"At my age," she had said one day to Alexia, "I should have by now half a dozen grandchildren to spoil, but that tiresome son of mine does not look like giving me even one until I shall be too old to hold it."

Alexia also thought it was a pity that the Marquis lived alone in this huge house and there were no children to play "hide-and-seek" in the Castle.

Mr. Dugdale had shown her pictures which had been painted of the ancestral seat of the Osmintons for nearly eight centuries.

The Castle had first been built in Norman times. It had been demolished and burnt down, and yet always, like a phoenix, it had sprung up again on the same site surrounded by the Osminton lands, which had grown and extended all down the centuries.

Now it was a magnificent building and Alexia longed to have a chance of seeing it.

Then she told herself it was no use entertaining hopes. When the Season was over they would return to Bedfordshire; at least that would be her and Peter's fate!

Perhaps Letty would find a suitable husband and would escape the monotony of the flat countryside and the long winters when day after day they shivered and saw nobody.

She was still looking at the Dowager Marchioness's portrait when the Marquis came back into the room.

"I thought you had gone to bed," he said.

"There is . . . something I want to . . . say to you first."

"Not another problem I have to solve?"

"I-it was . . . clever of you . . . so very, very clever of you to f-find Peter," Alexia said, "and once again I have no . . . words in which to express . . . my gratitude."

"Are you telling me that your vocabulary is somewhat limited?" the Marquis asked. "That is not the impression other people have of you, Alexia."

"To say what is in . . . one's mind is one thing," Alexia answered. "It is far more . . . difficult to express what is in one's . . . heart."

She was saying quite simply what she truly felt and he looked surprised as he handed her a glass of champagne which he poured out from a bottle resting in the silver ice-bucket.

"I think you need this," he said. "You have suffered quite a lot in the last half-hour."

"I would have suffered a . . . great deal more if it . . . had not been . . . for you."

She took a little sip of the champagne as if it gave her courage, then she put it down and said:

"There is . . . something I want to . . . to say to you."

"Shall we sit down?" the Marquis suggested.

"It will not take a moment," Alexia answered.

"It is just . . . that I want to ask you not to . . . let Peter ride . . . as you intend."

"You do not wish Peter to ride?" the Marquis asked. "Knowing what horses mean to him? And after what happened tonight?"

"You do not . . . understand," Alexia said. "It is just that I do not want to make him . . . dissatisfied with the life he will have to . . . lead in the future."

The Marquis did not speak but his eyes were on her face as she went on:

"In a few weeks this wonderful, incredible dream that is happening to Letty and me will be over, and Peter and I will be going back to Bedfordshire."

She paused, then as if she was choosing her words went on slowly:

"Once he has ridden your horses . . . how will he ever settle down to having some decrepit old pony, which will be all we can afford, or begging an occasional ride from the farmers who may be . . . kind enough to offer him one because they were . . . fond of Papa?"

"I suppose you yourself will not feel the contrast?" the Marquis suggested.

"Of course I shall feel it," Alexia answered, "but I shall have the good sense to be grateful, to understand that this is something that will never happen again. But how can I explain that to Peter?"

The Marquis did not answer and after a moment she said:

"I was wondering tonight if I had been . . . wrong in spending so much . . . time and money on Letty when there is also Peter to . . . consider. He has to be educated, but for the moment he will . . . have to make the best of Miss Graham and what I can . . . teach him."

"Suppose I . . . ?" the Marquis began.

"No!" Alexia said firmly. "I know what you are going to say. It is what Mr. Dugdale wanted to suggest just now, and I stopped him. We have taken so much that I refuse to accept any more."

"I thought you were fond of your brother."

"I am! You know I am!" Alexia said. "Tonight I felt . . ."

She stopped and the Marquis saw that the tears were back in her eyes. Then with an effort she went on:

"I have thrust myself upon you and have taken far more than I . . . ever intended when I first came here. But I still have my . . . pride, and because the same blood runs in the veins of both of us, my pride is no less strong than yours. I will not . . . allow Peter to be an . . . importunate relation."

He knew that as she spoke she was thinking of Mrs. Featherstone.

The Marquis finished his champagne and set the glass down on the tray.

"What I am going to suggest, Alexia," he said, "is that we leave these problems for the time being. You have been through quite an emotional experience this evening, which in any circumstances is inclined to throw one off balance."

Alexia made a little gesture with her hand, but she did not interrupt as the Marquis went on:

"I want you to go to bed. I believe my mother has plans for you and Letty tomorrow, and she will wish you to look your best. Forget about Peter for the moment. If you want to please me and show the gratitude that you say you feel towards me, then let him ride."

Alexia began to reply but the Marquis held up his hand to sweep her objections aside.

"If you knew that your brother was a genius as a musician," he said, "would you forbid him to be given a violin or be lent a pianoforte?"

Alexia did not answer and he continued in a serious voice:

"I think that Peter is a genius when it comes to horses. Perhaps in the future it may prove greatly to his advantage. I do not think either you or I would be able to sleep peacefully at night if we thought we were denying him the opportunity of being uniquely successful in this particular way, if in no other."

Alexia clasped her hands together.

"That sounds very . . . convincing, My Lord, and quite . . . frankly, I do not . . . know what to say."

"Then suppose you leave it to me?" the Marquis suggested. "I will look after Peter as my mother is looking after you and Letty, and because I was a boy myself it is a position for which I feel I am well qualified."

He was smiling, but Alexia's eyes were full of tears.

"You are . . . right," she said in a very low voice, "my vocabulary is . . . hopelessly . . . limited!"

The tears overflowed and ran down her cheeks. As if she wanted to hide them she turned and ran from the room.

Chapter Five

The Marquis having finished a large breakfast picked up *The Times* and started to read the head-lines.

The sun was shining in through the windows of the Morning-Room, which also overlooked the garden but at a different angle from the Library.

The door opened and Mr. Dugdale came in with the letters that had arrived by post.

The Marquis put down *The Times*.

"Good-morning, Dugdale," he said. "I hope you slept well after such a disturbed night?"

"I went to bed full of admiration for Your Lordship's quick grasp of the situation," Mr. Dugdale replied. "I cannot imagine why I had not thought of looking in the stables."

"I can still hardly believe what happened," the Marquis said reflectively. "I was always fond of horses myself as a small boy, but I was certainly not as fearless as Peter appears to be."

"I think just as gardeners have what they call a 'green thumb,'" Mr. Dugdale smiled, "there are people who have a magical way with animals."

"Like lion-tamers, I suppose," the Marquis said, and laughed.

He changed the subject by putting out his hand for the letters which Mr. Dugdale had brought in.

"Is there anything important in the post?"

"Nothing that I cannot deal with, My Lord, except for this."

He held out an envelope which the Marquis recognised immediately was in Lady Harlow's hand-writing.

"Tear it up!" he ordered sharply. "And in the future do not even bother to bring them to me."

"Very well, My Lord."

Mr. Dugdale hesitated for a moment, then he said:

"I understand Your Lordship went to Royal Avenue last evening. I hope everything was to your satisfaction?"

"Very much so!" the Marquis answered.

He was about to change the conversation when something in his Comptroller's attitude struck him as peculiar.

He had relied on Mr. Dugdale for so long and they were so close in so many ways that just as his Comptroller anticipated his every need, so he often knew what he was thinking.

"What is wrong, Dugdale?" he asked.

"Nothing, My Lord, I was just a trifle anxious in case, as you had not let me inform *Mademoiselle* Duval that you were calling on her, she—might not be there."

The last words were spoken somewhat hesitatingly and the Marquis said sharply:

"Now let me have the truth. What did you really suspect?"

Mr. Dugdale did not reply and after a moment the Marquis said almost angrily:

"You know as well as I do, Dugdale, that if there is one thing that makes me annoyed it is veiled innuendoes. I think you know me well enough to tell me the truth, whatever it may be."

"It is only something I read, My Lord."

"What did you read?"

Again Mr. Dugdale hesitated, then he said:

"It was in one of the more scurrilous newspapers, and was doubtless untrue, but it hinted that

93

Mademoiselle Duval is enamoured of an actor who is playing the lead in *The Country Girl*."

The Marquis thought for a moment and remembered seeing on the stage a handsome young man who had recently taken over the part of an older and more experienced actor.

He was just about to say that theatrical gossip was even more unreliable than that which was circulated about the members of the *Beau Ton,* when something came to his mind.

He had last night had a bath before dinner in Royal Avenue.

The fact that he had installed one in the house he owned in Chelsea had been the delight of every Fair Charmer whom he had taken under his protection.

It opened out of Renée's bed-room, and the Marquis thought, as he had often done before while bathing, that the comfort as far as he was concerned was well worth the expense.

As he had dried himself he noticed that on a table by the basin there was a razor in a leather case.

With its ivory handle it was exactly the same as those he used, and he thought it was typical of the consideration and attention to detail which the Frenchwomen brought to their love-affairs that Renée should have provided one for him in case he should need it.

As it happened the Marquis, like Napoleon Bonaparte, shaved himself, while the majority of the aristocracy relied upon their valets or on professional barbers.

He had also before dinner tied his cravat with an experienced hand that infuriated his valets, who liked to think themselves indispensable.

Now, looking back, he remembered that when he went to the bathroom again the razor had vanished.

He had hardly noticed it at the time, any more than later when he left the house he had not thought it strange when the maid who saw him out said:

"We are getting a little short of champagne and claret, M'Lord."

"I will see to it," the Marquis answered vaguely, telling himself he would give the order to his Comptroller in the morning.

Now it struck him that it was not so very long ago that he had sent quite a number of cases of both wines to Chelsea.

Renée, unlike many of her profession, drank very little.

When she had supper with the Marquis she would drink only perhaps two glasses from a bottle of champagne and always refused the exotic liqueurs which were the delight of chorus-girls.

The Marquis felt his temper rising.

It was not that he really blamed Renée for forming another attachment when he had admittedly neglected her in the past month.

But it was obvious, he thought now, that her almost overwhelming flattery and her continual repetition of her delight in seeing him were due to a guilty conscience.

It was understood that when a woman became the acknowledged mistress of a protector who not only installed her in a house and paid all the expenses but also, as in Renée's case, provided her with a carriage, she kept her favours exclusively for him.

The Marquis was conceited enough to believe, rightly or wrongly, that he had not been deceived in the past—at least he had never been suspicious.

But now he was aware that he was being made a fool of by another man. It was a new sensation which he did not enjoy.

"I think, Dugdale," he said at last after a long silence, "*Mademoiselle* Duval should receive the usual cheque with a notice to leave the house within a month."

There was no expression of any sort in the Marquis's voice and Mr. Dugdale answered briefly:

"It shall be seen to, My Lord."

"I would like to read that letter from Newmarket again," the Marquis went on in a very different tone. "I did not have time to study it carefully yesterday and there are several points I wish to raise with you."

"I will fetch it immediately, My Lord," Mr. Dugdale replied.

* * *

Upstairs, Letty, who had been called at what seemed to her a very late hour, was sitting up in bed enjoying her breakfast.

It was one of the delights of living at Osminton House that the breakfast-trays looked so attractive and the dishes were so appetising that they made for both Letty and Alexia an exciting start to the day.

They had been warned by Mr. Dugdale that the Marquis disliked female company early in the morning and were only too ready to agree that they should breakfast in their own rooms.

On Letty's tray now there was not only a covered silver dish but a plate containing huge purple muscat grapes from the gardens at Osminton Castle and a peach which was bigger than the balls which Peter played with.

She sat up against the pillows to pour out the fragrant coffee, and with her fair hair framing her perfect skin she looked very lovely as Alexia came into the room.

"Did you sleep well, dearest?" she asked.

"Like a top!" Letty answered. "I thought I would be too excited to do so, but I can hardly remember getting into bed and the next thing I knew it was morning!"

There was a note in her voice that told Alexia without words that something unusual had happened.

"Was there anything very special to make you so excited?" she asked.

Letty did not answer for a moment as her mouth

was full, and Alexia seated herself on the end of the bed.

"I have a suspicion that you are hiding something from me," she said.

"Let me finish this delicious dish while it is hot," Letty pleaded, "then I have something to tell you."

Alexia waited, thinking as she did so that Letty seemed to grow more beautiful every day.

'It is because she is having plenty of the right food, besides being happy,' she thought.

She wondered what would happen if when the Season came to an end Letty had not found a suitable husband and would have to return to the discomforts of Bedfordshire.

'She must make the best of her chances,' Alexia thought.

Then she felt tense with the anxiety which never really left her mind.

Letty put down her knife and fork.

"That was delicious!" she said. "Now I am going to eat the peach. Would you like half of it?"

"No, thank you. I have had one already," Alexia answered, "and I am very impatient to hear what you have to tell me."

Letty picked up the peach and started to peel it.

"Do you promise on your honour to say nothing to anyone?"

"Of course!" Alexia answered. "If you ask me not to do so."

"And especially—most especially—to the Marquis?"

"What is all this?"' Alexia asked. "You know as well as I do I would never reveal anything you told me, and especially, as you say, to the Marquis."

Letty gave a little sigh, then she said:

"I think, Alexia, I am in love!"

"In love?" Alexia repeated. "With whom?"

It flashed through her mind, because of what Letty had said, that it might be the Marquis. Then before she could frame the question Letty went on:

"He told me last night that he loves me, and that he had never seen anyone like me before in his life. Oh, Alexia, he says such wonderful things!"

"Who does? Who are you talking about?" Alexia asked.

"The Duke of Gleneagles!" Letty answered.

"The Duke of Gleneagles?" Alexia exclaimed. "I do not remember him. Where did we meet him?"

"Not you—me!" Letty said. "I met him a week ago! He introduced himself to me at the Ball given by the Duchess of Bedford."

"He introduced himself?" Alexia repeated. "Surely that was unusual?"

"He explained why later," Letty said. "He has quarrelled with the Marquis and his mother does not get on with the Dowager Marchioness."

"Does he want to marry you?" Alexia asked.

"I know he does! He has not actually said so, but it is obvious from the things he says! Oh, Alexia, he worships me!"

"Then if he really loves you," Alexia said quickly, "he will have to ask the Marquis's permission to marry you. After all, we are here as his guests and he is head of the family, so that would be the correct way to behave."

"I doubt if Euan will behave correctly," Letty replied with a smile. "He is very masterful and determined to have his own way."

"Supposing the Marquis refuses?"

"I see no reason why he should do that," Letty said slowly. "After all, it would be a brilliant marriage!"

"Just the sort I have always longed for you to have," Alexia agreed, "and of course with someone you love."

"Euan says the most thrilling things," Letty said, and sighed. "He thinks I look like a goddess and he says that he wants to kiss me from the top of my lovely head to the soles of my tiny feet!"

"Letty!"

Alexia was shocked.

"You should not allow any man to talk to you like that unless you are engaged to him."

"We are really engaged," Letty replied. "Euan says he cannot live without me. There are difficulties where the Marquis is concerned, but he says he will explain them to me in detail the next time we meet."

Alexia did not speak and she went on:

"You see, because of this stupid feud—I do not know what it is about—when we meet at parties we dare not dance openly if the Dowager Marchioness is there, or the Marquis. So we have to slip away into the garden."

She smiled and went on:

"It is not very difficult. Last night we found a little arbour hidden away where no-one would have thought to look for us."

"Letty, that is very improper, as you well know! If Her Ladyship learnt about it she would be very angry."

"Why should I worry what she feels about Euan?" Letty asked petulantly. "You know what these old families are like—always having quarrels that go on for generation after generation. It is too ridiculous! Euan says so himself."

"But he cannot marry you without asking the Marquis's permission," Alexia said firmly. "Would you like me to speak to him about it?"

Letty gave a cry and nearly upset her breakfast-tray.

"No, no, Alexia! You promised me—you promised you would say nothing."

"And of course I will keep my word," Alexia said soothingly, "but I am only trying to make things easier for you."

"I can manage everything quite well for myself," Letty said in a voice which made Alexia look at her in surprise.

Letty had never managed anything for herself.

She was one of those amenable people who always

did what she was told, who always agreed with everyone else.

Sometimes in the past, in spite of the fact that she loved her younger sister so overwhelmingly, Alexia had found this irritating.

But for Letty to speak to her now in such a manner was almost revolutionary.

"Now listen, darling," she said. "You have to be sensible about this. We owe the Marquis everything, and I think it is wrong, very wrong, to deceive him."

Letty considered this for a moment, then she said:

"Perhaps you are right, Alexia. I had not thought of it like that."

"Think what he has given us! Think what we are enjoying at his expense," Alexia went on. "His mother is chaperoning us, we have the most fabulous clothes that any girls could dream of, we are staying here, and entirely thanks to him you have been acclaimed as the most beautiful débutante of the Season."

"I do see that it would be very ungrateful to do anything he does not like," Letty said after a moment. "But supposing he says I am to give up Euan?"

"Why should he say anything of the sort?" Alexia asked. "After all, it is you who are to marry him!"

"Perhaps when the time comes," Letty said hopefully, "he would be glad to have one of us at any rate off his hands."

"I am sure that is the ... truth," Alexia agreed, thinking of the trouble Peter had caused last night.

"I will tell you what I will do," Letty said. "I shall see Euan tonight, since we have arranged to meet at the Ball—I cannot remember who is giving it—and I will tell him what you said."

"Please do that," Alexia answered. "And I love you, Letty, for being so sensible."

"The Marquis and his mother have been very, very kind," Letty reiterated. "I suppose if I had not had such beautiful gowns neither Euan nor anybody else would have admired me."

"Your face would still have looked lovely," Alexia answered, "but you know as well as I do we would both have appeared like Cinderellas amongst all those smartly dressed women with their fine jewellery."

"I am grateful—I am!" Letty exclaimed. "But I do think it is tiresome that of all the men who have paid court to me, Euan, who is much the nicest, should have quarrelled with the Marquis."

"Did he say it was a very serious quarrel?" Alexia enquired.

"He said that the Marquis would try to prevent us from meeting and so would his mother," Letty replied, "but really there was not time to say any more."

"But you have been seeing him every evening?"

"Nearly every evening, except for last Thursday when he was not asked to the Ball we attended. Can you imagine anything so annoying? But I was not too disappointed, because he had warned me that he would not be there."

"How do you communicate with him?" Alexia asked.

Letty looked at her rather apprehensively.

"You may be angry with me when I tell you."

"I promise you I will not," Alexia replied.

"Well, he gave me money with which to bribe one of the footmen."

"Oh, Letty!" Alexia exclaimed reproachfully.

"I said you might be angry," Letty said, "but Euan was afraid, and so was I, of Mr. Dugdale. He sees the post as soon as it arrives and might tell the Marquis that Euan was writing to me."

"I cannot believe that Mr. Dugdale would open our letters," Alexia said.

"One never knows," Letty answered vaguely, "and Euan is absolutely insistent that I should tell no-one, not even you, that we care for each other."

"Did he really say that you should not tell me?" Alexia asked.

"I cannot exactly remember," Letty replied, "but

I think so. Anyway, he impressed on me that what we feel for each other must be a complete and absolute secret."

Letty smiled happily before she added:

"But you know I cannot keep any secrets from you. I have been wanting to tell you every day, but I was not quite certain until last night that Euan really loved me."

"Then what are you going to do?" Alexia asked.

She was in fact worried and rather appalled by what Letty had told her.

It was certainly extremely unfortunate that Letty should think herself in love with someone of whom the Marquis disapproved.

But it seemed inconceivable that he would try to prevent Letty from making what would obviously be a brilliant marriage.

At the same time, she felt the Marquis would have a sensible reason for any animosity he might feel towards a man, Duke or otherwise.

Alexia had learnt that where Letty was concerned she would always respond if one appealed to her better nature.

It would therefore be a mistake for her to say firmly and categorically that she must find out exactly what objections the Marquis had to the Duke and that if they were valid she would have to give him up.

Instead she said aloud:

"You know, dearest, that all I want is your happiness, and it seems too wonderful that you should fall in love with someone so important. At the same time, it would spoil it all if you were to do anything to anger or upset the Marquis."

Letty did not speak and after a moment Alexia said:

"I rather wondered why you had not . . . fallen in love . . . with him."

"I did when I first saw him," Letty said. "He was so magnificent, so handsome! But it would be very

dull to be married to a man who thinks he is being
condescending if he takes off his hat to you."

Alexia laughed, she could not help it.

Letty said such funny, droll things in all serious-
ness, and Alexia understood what she meant.

The Marquis did indeed appear to condescend
even when he obeyed his mother and escorted them to
one of their evening engagements.

"You will speak to the Duke this evening, will
you not, Letty?" she asked. "Explain that you cannot
go on meeting him secretly unless you know why
there has to be so much secrecy about it."

"I will tell him," Letty said.

Then as she finished the peach she was eating she
lay back against the pillows and said:

"It is so wonderful when men look at me with a
swimmy look in their eyes and find it difficult to put
into words how lovely they think I am."

Alexia did not answer and Letty went on:

"They kiss my hand, but I know they are longing to kiss my lips, though often they are too shy to
suggest it."

Alexia's back stiffened.

"Are you telling me, Letty, that you have been
kissed?"

"Yes, of course!" Letty answered. "But only when
I like a man very much."

"But, Letty, that is extremely improper!" Alexia
exclaimed. "You should never allow any man to kiss
you until you are engaged to him."

"You did not tell me that before," Letty said lightly.

"I thought you knew it would be wrong."

"Why should I know anything of the sort?" Letty
asked. "It did not seem wrong to me, but very nice.
They get so excited and say things like: 'God, you are
wonderful!' "

"What you want them to say is: 'Will you marry
me?' " Alexia retorted.

"Two men have said that," Letty replied.

"Why did you not tell me?" Alexia asked.

"I did not like them," Letty answered. "One was old, rather like that horrible man who was running after you, and the other was a very stupid boy. He had so little chin that it disappeared inside his collar!"

"But . . . Letty . . ." Alexia began.

Then she knew that everything she had planned when they came to London was falling about her ears.

Alexia had decided that Letty must find a husband, and somehow, because her younger sister had always done what she wanted her to do, she had never envisaged that Letty would have an opinion of her own on the matter.

Now she told herself that Letty had grown up overnight and was refusing proposals of marriage without even bothering to tell her about them.

'It is my fault,' Alexia thought humbly.

She had gone ahead with her plans almost as if Letty were not a human being capable of thinking for herself.

Then it struck her that perhaps Letty had been cleverer than she gave her credit for. She had found herself a Duke, and if he really wanted to marry her, what could be a more wonderful and perfect ending to a fairy-story?

"Promise me, dearest," Alexia said now, "that you will speak to the Duke tonight and find out the truth. And, if it is at all possible, please introduce him to me."

"I cannot introduce you tonight," Letty answered.

"Why not?"

"Because you and I are not going to the same party."

"What do you mean?"

"The Dowager Marchioness told me yesterday that her friend Lady Blessington is giving a small dance for young people and has too many girls already. So, while I am going there, you are going with the Dowager Marchioness to a Reception at Carlton House."

"At Carlton House? Why did nobody tell me?" Alexia asked. "Oh, Letty, that must be very disappointing for you."

"Not in the slightest!" Letty answered. "I saw that fat old Regent the other night and was presented to him. I cannot think why everybody makes such a fuss about him!"

Alexia said nothing. She could understand that Letty found the Regent, who was forty-eight, very old.

At the same time, she herself had found him charming and could understand the fascination which made the Marquis call him a friend.

"Well, perhaps I can meet the Duke tomorrow night," Alexia said.

"I will tell him that you want to meet him," Letty replied. "At the same time, he may be annoyed that I have broken my promise not to tell anyone."

"It is something which cannot be kept a secret forever," Alexia said firmly.

Even as she spoke she thought that time was getting on. It was true that the Season was to extend until after the Regent's Fête on June 19, for which the invitations had already arrived.

But she felt as if every day the grains of sand in the hour-glass were running down until finally nothing would be left.

She was just about to warn Letty again and beg her to behave in a more circumspect fashion, when Letty threw back the bed-clothes and jumped out of bed.

"It is a lovely day, and I am happy—so very, very happy!" she cried.

She put her arms round her sister, hugged her, and kissed her cheek.

"Who would ever have imagined or even dreamt that the Social World could be full of so many excitements," she asked, "and such heavenly, marvellous things to do?"

She looked at the worried expression on her sister's face and added:

"Do not be cross with me, Alexia, I will not do anything else naughty, I promise you. I will just marry Euan and live happily ever afterwards."

"That is what I hope you will do, dearest," Alexia answered.

But there was just a touch of doubt in her voice.

*   *   *

Everything that was happening, Alexia told herself, made her feel, as Letty did, that the world was a marvellous place and full of sunshine.

Yet as she looked round Carlton House and thought it was more fantastic than she had even imagined, she was thinking of Letty and wondering if she was being firm with the Duke.

From the moment she had entered the splendid Hall decorated with Ionic columns of brown sienna marble and proceeded up the graceful double staircase beside the Dowager Marchioness and the Marquis, she knew that this was something to remember for the rest of her life.

The Marquis had told them in the carriage driving from Park Lane that this was to be one of the small dinner-parties at which the Regent entertained his personal friends.

As he spoke he remembered how Imogen had pleaded with him to get her invited, and he told himself he was glad that his companions this evening were his mother and Alexia.

He could rely on the latter to behave with propriety and listen intelligently to whoever conversed with her.

Glancing at the guests who were already assembled in the Drawing-Room, which was decorated in the Chinese taste, Alexia realised that she was the youngest person present and in fact the only unmarried woman.

The rest of the party included of course Lady

Hertford, splendidly attired with magnificent jewels, and a number of ladies who seemed to Alexia to be as old or rather middle-aged.

She was, however, for the moment more interested in the house itself than its occupants.

She had learnt from Mr. Dugdale that she must look out for the fine Van Dykes which the Prince had bought and thereby added to his debts, and numerous other fine English and Dutch pictures which had also contributed their astronomical amount.

But there was much more than pictures to see, Alexia discovered.

She found herself bewildered by the furnishings, the Gobelin tapestries, the Sèvres china, the cabinets, the chests, and the marble busts, all of which she longed to have the time to examine quietly and without being interrupted.

But she knew that having been honoured by such an invitation she must "sing for her supper" by making herself agreeable.

She therefore listened wide-eyed and attentively at dinner to the gentlemen on either side of her.

They both found it surprisingly easy to talk to her and both before the evening was over congratulated the Marquis on having such a clever as well as beautiful Ward.

The Regent, now that he was getting older, did not keep the late hours that he had done when he was a young man and they left Carlton House soon after 11:30 P.M.

They arrived back in Park Lane long before there was any chance, Alexia knew, of Letty returning home from her party.

The Marquis had not accompanied them further than White's Club. As he stepped out in Saint James's Street his mother admonished him:

"Do not lose too much money on the green baize tables, Chilton. I can always think of a so much better use for it."

"As it happens I am usually a winner," the Marquis replied, "which of course, Mama, you will undoubtedly interpret as an omen of being unlucky in love!"

The Dowager Marchioness had smiled a little ruefully, and when the carriage door shut behind him she said to Alexia:

"I cannot think why men, and women too for that matter, find gambling so attractive. The Duchess of Devonshire, of whom I was so fond, absolutely ruined her health and her looks by her preoccupation with the cards."

"If I had any money," Alexia said, "I would certainly not risk it in such a foolish manner."

"You and I think the same," the Dowager Marchioness replied, "but men can never resist a challenge. I often think that what my son needs is more obstacles to overcome—more mountains to climb, if you like to put it in that way."

"I can quite understand," Alexia said with a smile. "The trouble with His Lordship is that he is too good at everything: he wins the races, he gains at cards, he has the admiration of everyone who sees him. What more has he to achieve?"

"I can answer that in one word," the Dowager Marchioness said. "Love!"

Alexia looked startled and she went on to explain:

"I am quite convinced that my son has never really been in love. Oh, there have been numerous women in his life. That is understood. He is far too attractive for them to leave him alone."

She sighed and went on:

"What I want, what I pray for every night, is that he will fall in love and know the happiness my husband and I enjoyed together."

The words gave Alexia a strange feeling in her breast that she could not explain to herself.

She was, however, so ignorant about love that there was nothing she could say except murmur sympathetically.

Back at Osminton House, she kissed the Dowager Marchioness good-night and thanked her for what she knew would always be a memorable evening, then she went to her own room.

She thought as she got into bed that she would doubtless hear Letty returning and she would go and ask her what had happened.

But she was more tired than she knew and did not stir until nine o'clock the next morning, when the maid came in to draw back the curtains and bring in her breakfast.

"Is Miss Letty awake yet?" Alexia asked, feeling that it was unlikely.

"No, Miss. There's a note outside her door saying she does not wish to be disturbed until she rings."

'That means she must have been very late,' Alexia thought.

It was hard to restrain her impatience to talk to her sister.

She bathed, dressed, and went up to the Nursery to find Peter ready to go riding and in his usual state of excitement about it.

"Sam says that I handle Hercules as if I were a man," he said, "and today we are going to gallop even faster than we did yesterday!"

"That will be lovely!" Alexia smiled. "Do not forget when you see the Marquis to thank him for letting you ride such a magnificent horse."

"I have thanked him," Peter said.

"Then you must go on thanking him every time you see him," Alexia admonished. "It is not every man, Peter, who would let you ride his horses, however many he had!"

"He has lots I have not seen," Peter said, "and Sam says he is buying more. Why have we not enough money to buy lots of horses?"

"Perhaps you will have when you grow up," Alexia retorted, "but you will have to be clever and make the money to buy them."

"I will make money if it means I can buy horses,"
Peter said.

Then impatiently he said to Miss Graham:

"Oh, come on, Gra-Gra! You are so slow! Sam
will be waiting for me."

"I will take Peter to the stables," Alexia said.

"That would be kind of you, Miss Alexia," Miss
Graham answered. "I have got a headache this morning and feel as if my fingers are all thumbs."

"You must lie down," Alexia said, "and when
Peter comes home I will give him his luncheon and
take him out with me this afternoon."

"That is very kind of you," Miss Graham answered, "but I shall be all right. It is just that I 'got
out of bed the wrong side' this morning, as my mother
used to say."

'She is very kind,' Alexia thought to herself. 'At
the same time, she is too old.'

She wondered if the Marquis had forgotten saying that Peter needed a Tutor and he would see to it.

Then she rebuked herself for being so grasping as
to expect more from him when they had taken so
much already.

She and Peter hurried to the stables through the
garden and when Peter had ridden off, looking very
small and yet somehow extremely confident on the
back of Hercules, she returned to the house.

She went upstairs, and, realising how late it was,
she thought Letty must now be awake.

But the notice was still on the floor outside her
bed-room and Alexia went to see the Dowager Marchioness.

There was nothing the Dowager liked more than
chattering over what had happened the night before.

She had something to relate about everyone who
had been at the dinner-party and she made Alexia
laugh with stories of their backgrounds and their ancestors.

When it was time for the Dowager Marchioness

to be getting up, Alexia said a little hesitantly, trying
to make her voice sound very casual:

"Someone last night spoke of the Duke of Gleneagles, Ma'am. I do not seem to have met him at any
of the Balls and I wondered if you knew him."

"The Duke of Gleneagles?" the Dowager Marchioness repeated. "I believe he is in London. I have
seen him in the distance on one or two occasions."

She smiled, then she said:

"Do not set your cap in that direction, my dear.
He would be no use to either you or Letty, and that
is why I have not asked him to any of our dinner-
parties."

"Why would he be no use?" Alexia asked, trying
not to appear to be inquisitive.

"He is to be married next month to the Earl of
Berwick's daughter, and a very suitable match it will
be, the two families being of great consequence in the
North. The Duke and his future bride have known
each other ever since they were children."

Alexia felt her heart stand still, then the Dowager
Marchioness said:

"I will tell you a secret that will amuse you. Lady
Berwick told me herself that her naughty daughter
and the young Duke were so impatient to be married
and bored with the long-winded family discussions
about it that they had wed each other by the ancient
ceremony of Marriage by Consent."

"What is . . . that?" Alexia managed to ask through
dry lips.

"In Scotland," the Dowager Marchioness explained
"two people have only to declare before witnesses
that they are man and wife and they are in fact legally
espoused!"

She laughed.

"Of course the noble families consider it a most
reprehensible way to behave, and it is in fact seldom
used these days except when the bride is with child."

She laughed again before she added:

"I am sure there is nothing like that about Elspeth. It was just a prank to stop their relations yattering and to make them get down to business. But it means that legally the Duke is at this moment a married man, and therefore, you understand, dearest child, I saw no point in entertaining him on your or Letty's behalf."

"N-no . . . Ma'am," Alexia agreed.

At the same time, she felt almost faint at the horror of what she had heard.

She left the Dowager Marchioness's room and walked determinedly towards Letty's.

However tired her sister might be, she would wake her up and tell her what she had discovered.

No wonder, she thought angrily, the Duke had pledged Letty to keep their relationship a secret from the Marquis.

His behaviour was extremely reprehensible and, what was more, Alexia thought, positively cruel.

He might easily have broken Letty's heart, and although she did not think that this would happen, feeling that her sister was not as emotionally involved as Letty herself thought, yet it would be a blow to her pride.

The last thing Alexia wanted was for Letty to fall into a state of melancholy when, as she had said yesterday morning everything was so wonderful and she was so happy.

The note was still outside Letty's room but she opened the door and went in.

The room was in darkness and she crossed to the window to pull back the curtains. The sun came streaming in and she turned to look at the bed.

It had been slept in but Letty was not there.

She was just about to go to her own room, thinking that Letty must have awakened and gone in search of her, when she saw an envelope lying on the dressing-table. It was inscribed ALEXIA.

She picked it up, feeling for the moment that it

112

was impossible to open it, impossible to read what was inside.

When she did open it, for a moment Letty's round, rather childish writing danced in front of her eyes before she could read:

> *Dearest Alexia,*
>
> *Because Euan thinks there will be so much trouble and disagreeableness about our being together, I have decided to run away with him. We are going to be married in Dover and sail in his yacht along the South Coast towards Land's End. It will be quite safe because the English ships have routed Napoleon's and are guarding the Channel.*
>
> *Do not worry about me, because I am so happy, and please ask the Marquis and his mother not to be cross.*
>
> *Your loving and devoted*
Letty

Alexia read the letter through twice, then she closed her eyes.

"What am I to do?" she asked herself. "Oh, God, what am I to do?"

Chapter Six

Alexia knew that the only person who could help her would be the Marquis, and, holding Letty's letter in her hand, she ran down the stairs to the Hall.

"Where is His Lordship?" she enquired of a footman.

"His Lordship's gone riding, Miss," the man replied, "and won't be back for an hour or so."

"And Mr. Dugdale?"

"Mr. Dugdale has also gone out, Miss, but he should be back afore luncheon."

Alexia felt frantic, knowing that Letty, having left for Dover, must somehow be prevented from sailing away in the Duke's yacht.

She thought despairingly that he would think up some plausible explanation as to why they could not, as Letty expected, be married before they set out to sea—and then it would be too late!

For a moment Alexia felt as if her brain would not function and was full of cotton-wool.

Then resolutely she walked into the Library, sat down at the Marquis's desk, pulled a piece of his writing-paper towards her, and tried to think what she should say.

Because time was passing and she felt sure he would understand without explanations, she just scribbled:

*"I have gone to Dover. Please, please help me!
Alexia."*

She thrust the piece of paper into an envelope and
with it Letty's letter. Then she ran upstairs, put on the
first bonnet she took from the cupboard, and snatched
up a light silk cloak which she wore when travelling.

She went down again and by now realised that it
was important that no-one but the Marquis should
know what had happened. She instructed one of the
footmen:

"Will you tell Her Ladyship if she asks for me that
I had to see a friend? His Lordship will explain when
he returns. Please inform His Lordship that I have
left a note for him on his desk."

"Very good, Miss," the footman answered. "Will
you require a carriage?"

"I will go to the stables myself," Alexia replied.

She knew it would be intolerable to wait even
the few minutes it would take for a carriage to be
brought round to the front door.

She went back through the Library and ran
across the lawn towards the door in the wall, remembering how the Marquis had brought Peter home in
triumph after he had disappeared.

"He will help me to save Letty—I know he will!"
Alexia told herself as she ran.

She reached the Mews and found to her relief that
Sam was there.

"I have to reach Dover, Sam, in the quickest possible time."

The groom looked at her in surprise. Then she said:

"It is urgent, desperately urgent! We have to catch
up with the Duke of Gleneagles."

The groom looked at her with understanding in
his eyes. Then he said:

" 'Is Grace the Duke of Gleneagles, unless I'm
mistaken, 'll be driving 'is Phaeton with two horses.
They're fine enough, but not t' be compared with
'is Lordship's team."

"Please, Sam, let us take those," Alexia pleaded.

"I don't know, Miss, what 'is Lordship'll say," Sam replied.

Then, as if the expression in Alexia's eyes decided him, he said:

"We'll catch up with 'is Grace, don't you fear, Miss."

He snapped his fingers and the stable-boys came running.

In an incredibly short space of time the Marquis's team of black horses was between the shafts of what Alexia knew was a lightly sprung and very up-to-date travelling curricle.

By the time the horses were ready, Sam had put on his livery and his cockaded hat. He drove out of the Mews with an expertise which Alexia thought almost rivalled that of his master.

It did not take them long to reach the Dover road, where Sam gave the horses their heads as they passed through New Cross and Blackheath and on to Shooter's Hill.

It was difficult to talk at the speed at which they were travelling, but when they had covered what Alexia thought must be about ten miles she asked:

"Will we have to change horses?"

"Indeed we will, Miss, if we're t' keep up our speed," Sam replied. "Fortunately, 'is Lordship has 'is own horses stabled on all th' main roads."

Alexia gave a sigh of relief.

She knew this was the habit amongst the more wealthy aristocrats, but she had been afraid that perhaps the Marquis did not often travel to Dover.

That would have meant they would be obliged either to push their own horses to the point of exhaustion or change to the inferior animals that were normally obtainable in the Posting Inns.

They passed Gadds Hill, where there were still the skeletons of highwaymen rotting in their irons on the gibbets, and finally stopped at Rochester.

Knowing how quick Sam would be, Alexia sped

up the stairs of the old Inn, washed away the dust that had already accumulated on her face and hands, and had just time to drink a cup of coffee before once again they were on their way.

Although it was now time for her luncheon she did not feel hungry.

She was only conscious of a feeling of fear and agitation which was so acute, so poignant, that she felt as if it had settled in her breasts in a manner that was physically painful.

She tried to calculate how long it would be before the Marquis returned home, read her note, and decided what he should do about it.

She felt certain that he would not fail her and would follow her to Dover probably on horse-back, which would be considerably quicker than travelling in a vehicle on the main road.

"He is so wonderful!" Alexia said to herself. "He will contrive to save Letty somehow, as he saved us before."

Then as she felt her whole being reaching out towards him in a wordless cry for his assistance, she knew that she not only relied on him, she also loved him.

It was absurd, ridiculous, she told herself, to aspire to loving someone so important and so obviously immune both to her charms and to Letty's.

And yet she could not deny the feelings within herself, which she knew, if she was honest, had been there for a long time.

She had found it impossible when she was in a room with the Marquis not to be acutely conscious of him, not to feel her eyes continually straying in his direction.

She now admitted that when she woke up in the morning her first thought was of him, as was her last thought before she went to sleep at night.

She told herself it was just because he had been so kind and so generous that she wanted to please him.

But when she had put on the beautiful gowns which the Dowager Marchioness had given her, she knew there was only one person she hoped would notice her, only one man she wanted to admire her.

It was hopeless, like crying for the moon while knowing it was out of reach, and yet she told herself a little despairingly that it was inevitable that she, and Letty also, should fall in love with such a magnificently outstanding man.

She found it hard to understand how the Duke of Gleneagles or anyone else could attract Letty when if she compared them with the Marquis they must pale into insignificance.

But Letty had found him cold and unapproachable, while Alexia could only remember his kindness, his understanding, and the way he had carried Peter in his arms.

"I love him!" she told herself, and the wheels of the chaise seemed to be saying over and over again: "You love him! You love him!" as they drove on and on.

As they passed through the Medway Flats, Sam said:

"I thinks t'would be wise, Miss, for you t' have sommat t' eat when we change horses outside th' town."

"I am not hungry," Alexia replied. "They will make me a cup of coffee while I wash. That is all I need. But what about you?"

"I never eats nor drinks when I'm adriving, Miss," Sam replied with a grin. "I'd a good breakfast this morn. Me old woman sees t' that."

"How far ahead is His Grace?" Alexia asked with a little tremor in her voice.

She was quite sure that Sam would have made enquiries at the last Inn at which they had stopped.

"You don't want t' worry your head with mathematics, Miss," Sam answered. "I gathers His Grace'd a good start, but we're againing on 'im."

"You are sure of that?"

118

"Quite sure, Miss. We won't be far behind 'em by th' time we're in sight o' Dover."

Alexia had hoped they might overtake the Duke and Letty at Barham or one of the other small towns they would pass before they actually came to the Channel port.

She thought there would be a number of different Inns in Dover and time might be wasted while they went from one to another, trying to find Letty.

Alternatively, the Duke might drive straight to the Quay and they would be aboard the yacht and out of harbour before she could have contact with her sister.

When she thought this over she decided it was unlikely.

Letty would not only want to wash and have something to eat before they went aboard, but she was also expecting to be married.

The Duke would have some explaining to do unless he was prepared to commit bigamy.

'Oh, Mama,' Alexia cried in her heart, 'I must be in time—I must! How could this happen to Letty of all people?'

She knew it was because Letty was so good-humoured and so easily led that the Duke had been able to persuade her to set off on this mad escapade.

He would have made it sound romantic and exciting, and Letty had also said he was very determined to get his own way.

"How could he do anything so diabolical?" Alexia asked herself.

She knew the answer lay in the fact that Letty was so beautiful that it was not surprising that any man lost his head and wanted to possess her whatever the consequences.

On and on they went, and now at last, without having seen a sign of the Duke's Phaeton, they were nearing Dover.

They had been many hours on the road, but because she was so anxious and so keyed up Alexia did not feel tired, she was only frightened that she might be too late.

"Where do you think we will find His Grace?" she asked Sam.

She had never yet admitted to him that Letty was with the Duke, but she was quite certain he knew of it.

If he had not guessed why she was in such a hurry to reach Dover, he would doubtless have been told at the various Inns at which they had stopped that the Duke was not travelling alone.

"The King's Head be th' best an' be where 'is Grace always goes," Sam said.

"Then we will go there first," Alexia replied.

As they went over the downs towards the town, she had her first glimpse of the harbour.

She could see the masts of a large number of ships, and she prayed with even more intensity than she had done before that the Duke's yacht was still amongst them and not out on the open sea.

Now they were moving through the narrow streets and in a very short time saw the King's Head ahead of them.

Quite a number of carriages with their liveried coachmen were standing outside, and Alexia suddenly felt afraid and shy of going into the busy Hotel and asking for Letty.

Supposing the Duke had registered under a different name? Supposing he confronted her and refused to allow her to speak to her sister?

She had expected they would stop in the street outside the Hotel, but Sam drove the horses slowly and carefully through the open double doors which led into the yard at the back.

There were a number of smart vehicles, with the ostlers standing at their horses' heads, and Sam said in a note of satisfaction:

" 'Is Grace's 'ere, Miss. That be 'is Phaeton."

He pointed with his whip as he spoke and Alexia saw a Phaeton which was empty while the two steaming horses which had drawn it were in the charge of an ostler.

As if he knew what she was thinking, Sam said:

"If you'll wait 'ere, Miss, I'll see where 'is Grace is likely t' be."

"Could you do that, Sam?" Alexia asked gratefully.

Sam left the horses in the charge of two ostlers and walked in through the side door of the Inn.

He had only been gone a few minutes when a tall, handsome-looking man came out through the same door, walked across the yard, and got into the Phaeton which Sam had pointed out as belonging to the Duke.

Alexia held her breath.

This was the Duke of Gleneagles, she was sure, and he had left Letty in the Inn.

She watched him turn his horses and drive towards the exit.

As he passed an older and rather superior-looking ostler who was controlling the traffic in and out of the yard, Alexia heard him say:

"I shall be returning and will want stables for my horses."

The man touched his forelock.

"They'll be waiting for Your Grace."

The Phaeton drew out of the yard and Alexia jumped down from the curricule and hurried towards the entrance to the Hotel.

As she reached it she met Sam coming towards her.

"Miss Letty's in room number six, Miss," he said.

"Thank you, Sam."

Alexia walked quickly through the busy vestibule and without asking the way walked up the stairs as if she were a registered guest in the Hotel.

Nobody took any notice of her and she found herself in a narrow corridor with rooms opening off of it. She felt sure that Letty would be in the best of them, one which had a view towards the sea.

She was not mistaken. Number 6 was halfway down the corridor and she opened the door without knocking.

Letty was lying on the bed, fully dressed except for her bonnet, and her eyes were closed.

Alexia looked at her for a moment, then she turned and shut the door before she spoke.

"Letty!"

Her sister opened her eyes and gave a shrill cry.

"Oh, Alexia, Alexia! What are you doing here?"

"I followed you, dearest," Alexia said, walking towards the bed. "Letty, you cannot do this!"

Letty sat up and put out her arms like a child who needs comforting.

"Alexia, I am so glad you have come! I have been so foolish, and I know now I ought not to have run away without telling you."

"You ought not to have run away at all," Alexia said. "Listen to me, Letty, the Duke is already married!"

Alexia saw an expression of horror more than surprise on her sister's face, then Letty said:

"Oh, Alexia, take me home. I have been so stupid! I thought it would be so amusing and exciting to have a run-away marriage, but I am so tired, and we came at such a terrible speed that I feel sick."

Alexia held Letty close, knowing that she was nothing more than a child who had always clung to her when anything went wrong.

"Where has the Duke gone to?" she asked.

"He has gone to see if the yacht is ready to sail," Letty answered.

She held on to Alexia even more closely as she said:

"But I do not want to go with him—I have changed my mind. When he kissed me just now, Alexia, he—hurt me."

She put her fingers as she spoke up to her lips as if they were bruised.

"I do not like him—any more," she went on. "I want to go—home with you."

"I can understand that."

Letty gave a cry.

"Stop him, Alexia! Stop him from coming back. Lock the door and keep him out!"

Alexia rose from the bed.

"We will do that," she said. "I am sure it will not be long before the Marquis arrives."

"The Marquis? Did you tell him where I had gone?"

"I had to," Alexia answered. "I would have asked him to bring me, but he was out riding, and I felt I had to hurry to save you."

"I want to be safe. I do not want to marry the Duke now anyway," Letty said. "He hurt my lips and he held me too—tightly. I am—frightened, Alexia."

"It is all right," Alexia said soothingly. "He shall not hurt you again."

She turned the key in the door and found that there was also a wooden bolt. The door itself, however, looked rather frail, and after a moment she said:

"Get up, Letty, and help me to push this chest-of-drawers in front of the door, in case the Duke tries to break it down."

Letty gave an exclamation which was one of fear and jumped off the bed.

She helped Alexia pull the quite heavy oak chest-of-drawers in front of the door.

"That ought to keep him out," she said.

At the same time, she picked up a chair and put it on top of the chest and looked round to see if there was anything else they could add to the barricade.

"We must play for time," Alexia told her. "If he comes back, you must tell him to wait downstairs and you will be ready as soon as you can."

"Supposing he does not—believe me?" Letty asked.

She was frightened, and yet at the same time she

looked so exceedingly beautiful that Alexia could understand why the Duke was behaving in such a disgraceful manner.

She knew, however, that it was important to keep Letty calm.

"You have not washed your face, dearest," she said. "It is quite grey with dust, and your hair is covered too."

It she had meant to divert Letty's attention from the predicament they were in, she could not have chosen a better method.

She turned towards the mirror and gave an exclamation of horror at her appearance.

"Find my hair-brushes, Alexia," she said. "They are in the valise which the porter brought up when I arrived."

Alexia looked by the door and recognised a valise which they had brought with them to London. It was an old one but easy to carry.

She opened it and found that it contained several gowns packed not very skilfully by Letty, and there was also some underclothes, a nightgown, and her hairbrushes.

"Euan said he would buy me everything I wanted at every port we put into," Letty said in a small voice. "I brought what I thought I would—need for the first—night or so."

Alexia said nothing, but her lips tightened. She took the brushes out of the valise, carried them towards the dressing-table, and put them down by her sister.

Then Letty, who was sitting on the stool, reached out and caught her hand.

"You are not . . . angry with me, Alexia, for being so—deceitful, are you?" she asked.

"I think I am more hurt that you did not trust me," Alexia replied.

"I am sorry—I am really sorry," Letty said as the tears welled into her blue eyes.

She gave a little sob and went on:

"Euan made it sound such an adventure, and he was so positive that the Marquis would stop us from getting married just because he was spiteful and disagreeable. How did you know that he was—married already?"

"The Dowager Marchioness told me," Alexia said. "It was a prank. He and the girl to whom he was engaged were Married by Consent in Scotland."

Her voice was scathing as she went on:

"It is a ceremony which decent people in Scotland think slightly reprehensible, but it is absolutely legal and binding."

Letty was still for a moment; then, looking at her own reflection in the mirror, she said in a horrified tone:

"If—he had taken me away in his—yacht, as he intended—I—I would have been—his m-mistress!"

She gave a little cry and jumped up to throw her arms round her sister's neck.

"Forgive me, oh, dearest Alexia, forgive me! I know how foolish I have been, and it was very— naughty of me not to—tell you about Euan from the —very beginning."

Letty was crying tempestuously and Alexia held her close.

"It is all right now, dearest," she said. "I understand, and we must just forget about it."

"Supposing he will not—give me up? Supposing he—makes me go with him in his—yacht?"

"He will not do that," Alexia said, "and I know the Marquis will be here soon."

As she spoke, she thought that wherever he was, he must feel how greatly she needed him.

If Letty was inexperienced and ignorant of how men behaved in such circumstances, so was Alexia, and she felt it would be very uncomfortable to have a scene with the Duke, especially in a public place.

She knew too, although she was determined not to

say so, that if one word of this leaked out and was talked about by the social chatterboxes, it would ruin Letty's reputation.

It was obvious that her beauty and the fact that she was being sponsored by the Marquis had incurred a great deal of jealousy amongst the other débutantes, and such a tale would lose nothing in the telling.

"Everything will be all right," she said aloud. "Now stop crying, dearest, and wash your face."

Letty obeyed her automatically. While Alexia poured cold water from the ewer into the china basin, Letty washed her hands and face and brushed her hair.

"I feel better now," she said.

Even as she spoke they heard footsteps outside the door and her eyes widened in sudden fear.

"Say what I told you," Alexia said in a whisper.

There was a knock on the door.

"Who—who is it?" Letty asked in a quivering voice.

"It is I—Euan!"

"I—I am just changing," Letty said. "If you will —w-wait down—stairs—I—I—will be as quick as I can."

"Let me in!"

"No! No! I cannot!"

"Why not?"

"I—I—told you—I am—changing my g-gown."

"Let me help you."

"N-no! I will not be—long."

"Then hurry! We have to sail on the tide."

The Duke obviously waited a moment. Then, as Letty did not speak, he said:

"Let me in, Letty. I have something to tell you."

"I—c-cannot—I am not—d-decent."

"There is no need to be so modest with me."

Letty did not answer and the Duke said in a low voice:

"I have arranged for us to be married by the Captain of my yacht, so make yourself look beautiful for such an important occasion."

He moved away as he spoke and after a minute or so they heard his footsteps going down the uncarpeted oak staircase.

Letty drew a deep breath.

"He is a liar! A deceiver!" she exclaimed. "If it had not been for you, Alexia, I would have believed him."

She ran to her sister as she spoke and Alexia saw that she was trembling.

"It is all right, Letty," she said again. "He cannot hurt you. We just have to wait and pray that the Marquis will not be long."

They sat down side by side on the bed, Letty holding on tightly to Alexia's hand.

Slowly, so slowly that it seemed as if each one took a century, the minutes went by.

"He will come back! He will come back at any moment!" Letty said in a sudden panic. "Then he will force open the door."

"He will have to be very strong to do that," Alexia replied. "And it would make a scene in the Hotel. I cannot think he wants that."

"He says he—always—gets what he—wants," Letty said in a whisper.

"This time he is going to be disappointed," Alexia answered.

Time went on ticking slowly by, when suddenly again there were footsteps outside.

Letty gave a little cry of sheer terror and flung herself against Alexia.

There was a knock on the door.

Letty was quite incapable of speaking and Alexia thought there was no point in keeping up any further pretence.

"Who is it?" she called.

"Is that you, Alexia?" a voice replied, and pushing Letty aside Alexia sprang to her feet.

She ran across the room and pulled down the chair

127

and somehow without Letty's help managed to push the chest-of-drawers to one side. Then she unlocked and unbolted the door.

Outside, looking as elegant as if he had just come from Carlton House, stood the Marquis!

"You have . . . come!" Alexia said breathlessly.

"What else did you expect me to do?" the Marquis asked, walking into the room.

He looked at the chest-of-drawers and the chair with a faint smile, then walked to the bed, where Letty sat looking at him with frightened eyes.

"You certainly put everyone to a great deal of trouble, young woman!" he said rather sharply.

Letty was incapable of answering but her eyes filled with tears.

"She is very sorry," Alexia said quickly. "The Duke was very . . . persuasive."

The Marquis did not reply and Alexia said nervously:

"What . . . what have you d-done with him?"

"I have sent him back to London," the Marquis replied sharply, "with instructions to keep his mouth shut and never breathe a word of this to a living soul."

"He will . . . keep his promise?"

"If he does not I have threatened not only to call him out—and he is not particularly adept with a duelling-pistol—but also to inform the Earl of Berwick of his behaviour."

Alexia gave a sigh of relief.

"I felt sure that you would arrange things so that Letty would not lose her reputation."

"She certainly makes things very difficult," the Marquis replied, "but I dare say we can contrive between us to save her."

"What shall we do now?" Alexia asked.

"We will set off for London as soon as we have had something to eat and drink," the Marquis answered. "If Letty finds it tiring, she has no-one to blame but herself!"

"I—I am very—very sorry to have—been such a —n-nuisance," Letty said in a quivering voice.

"So you should be!" the Marquis replied sharply. "I am going downstairs now to order some food, and I suggest you both join me as quickly as you can."

"We will do that," Alexia said.

She looked at him and felt her heart sing with joy because he had come, because he had taken charge of everything.

Now she felt she had nothing to worry about, as everything was in the Marquis's hands; he was so capable, so proficient, that Letty was safe.

Without saying any more, the Marquis walked from the room, and Alexia said:

"Quick, Letty! Let us change into clean gowns. We do not want to look hot and dusty when we are dining with the Marquis."

"He is—angry with—me," Letty said unhappily.

"Then you must be charming and at the same time humble and contrite, and he will soon forgive you," Alexia advised.

She crossed the room to pull out of the valise the gowns Letty had packed and hang them up, shaking the creases out of them.

Fortunately, Alexia and Letty were similar in size and it was after only a little more than ten minutes that they walked demurely downstairs.

Letty was wearing the prettiest gown of a forget-me-not blue to match the colour of her eyes, and Alexia was dressed in pale green.

They left the valise repacked and fastened, ready for a porter to carry it downstairs.

As soon as they appeared, the Inn-keeper hurried forward to show them along a passage which led to a private Parlour.

He opened the door and they saw the Marquis standing in front of the fireplace, a glass of champagne in his hand.

"For females you have been surprisingly quick!"

There was a mocking note in his voice, but Alexia with a lift of her heart felt that he was no longer angry.

"You may serve the dinner now," he said to the Inn-keeper.

"Very good, M'Lord," the man answered.

He was just about to shut the door when the Marquis, looking past him into the vestibule, saw a gentleman speaking to one of the porters.

He walked from the room and when they were alone Letty said to Alexia:

"Do you think he is—still very—cross with me?"

Alexia shook her head.

"No, I am sure everything is all right. Just make yourself very pleasant, dearest, and I am certain all will be forgotten."

They waited for a few moments, then the Marquis came back into the Parlour, and to Alexia's surprise she saw that there was a gentleman following him.

He was an extremely distinguished-looking man of about the same age as the Marquis.

"I want to introduce an old friend of mine," the Marquis said to Alexia, "the Earl of Carthew!"

He turned to his friend with a smile.

"James, these are my cousins, Alexia and Letty Minton."

The Earl shook Alexia by the hand, then turned to Letty.

For a moment he was still and seemed incapable of speaking.

Alexia knew that this was what often happened when men saw Letty for the first time.

Then she realised that Letty was staring at the Earl in very much the same way as he was staring at her.

Afterwards, Alexia was able to look back and know that she had seen two people fall in love with each other at first sight so completely, so overwhelmingly, that there was no possible doubt that it had actually occurred.

The Marquis, quite unconscious of what was happening, had turned to where a bottle of champagne was resting in an ice-bucket.

"I am sure you need a drink, James," he was saying. "You must have had a tiring day."

He poured the champagne into three glasses and refilled his own, and as Alexia crossed the room to see if she could help him he said:

"My friend has been sent to Dover by the First Lord of the Admiralty to inspect some of His Majesty's Man-o'-War ships which are guarding the Channel."

"How interesting!" Alexia exclaimed.

"I have told him," the Marquis went on, "that we were here to see off one of our Minton relations who is sailing down the coast and along to Plymouth."

He glanced at Alexia to make sure she understood why he was telling her this, then went on:

"We would, of course, in the normal course of events have left earlier for London, but we were not certain whether our cousin would be able to sail on the turn of the tide. But now that she has done so, we must get home as soon as possible."

"Yes, of course," Alexia cried, thinking that the tale the Marquis had invented sounded very plausible.

Then as she picked up one of the glasses and carried it to Letty, she saw that her sister was paying no attention to anything they had been saying and was still looking at the Earl as if spellbound.

It was altogether a very strange dinner, Alexia thought later. She and the Marquis talked and the Earl joined in occasionally. But he found it hard to take his eyes from Letty.

She looked at him or glanced down shyly, looking so exquisitely beautiful as she did so that Alexia could understand why the Earl would often break off a sentence halfway through or ask to have repeated something the Marquis had said to him.

When finally dinner was finished and Alexia and

Barbara Cartland

Letty went upstairs to put on their bonnets and cloaks, Alexia said:

"You seem to find the Earl of Carthew very pleasant, Letty."

"He is the most attractive man I have ever seen!" Letty said in a dreamy voice. "Oh, Alexia, do you think he admires me?"

"I am sure he does!" Alexia answered.

"But how shall I see him again? Please, please ask the Marquis to invite him to Osminton House."

"I am sure he will do that," Alexia answered.

She felt the Marquis would not have missed the strangely instantaneous attraction of the two for each other.

She was therefore not surprised when, as they said good-bye to the Earl, he held Letty's hand for longer than was conventionally necessary.

"I shall see you tomorrow," Alexia heard him say in a low voice, and she saw Letty's eyes light up as he spoke.

* * *

There were cheers, and a cloud of rose-petals seemed to fill the air, as Letty and the Earl climbed into the open carriage and were driven away from Osminton House.

They were so much in love that the whole wedding-party seemed to be affected by it, and even the usual blasé and gossiping notabilities in the Church seemed touched as if by a magic spell.

As Letty had walked up the aisle on the Marquis's arm, with Alexia following them, she had not been surprised to see the Earl turn round to watch his bride approach and unconventionally take her hand as soon as she reached his side.

The expression of happiness in his face and the radiance in Letty's made many of the older women in the congregation wipe their eyes.

St. George's Hanover Square was redolent with the fragrance of lilies and Alexia thought that above the clear voices of the choir-boys she could hear the sound of angels.

She was quite certain in her heart that her mother was present and she felt that she was telling her it was everything she wanted for Letty and her future was assured.

They learnt that the Earl had been married before, when he was very young, but his wife had died without giving him any children, and, like the Marquis, he had meant to remain unmarried.

But Letty, he said frankly, was the embodiment of his dreams, and Alexia knew that he was just the sort of husband that her sister should have.

He was not only kind and considerate but protective. He would look after her and keep her safe, and that was what Letty needed above all else.

Because she had no girl-friends, Alexia had been her only bridesmaid, and Peter, with the Earl's nephew, who was the same age, had carried her train.

There had also been a number of the bridegroom's small nieces and cousins, who, dressed in pink, looked like a cluster of rose-buds as they followed Letty up the aisle.

It was not only an important wedding, it was also manifestly a happy one. And Alexia had had for the past weeks no time to think of herself or what would happen now that the Season had come to an end.

Letty's marriage had been hurried simply because the Earl wanted to take her to his estate in Oxfordshire for the start of their honeymoon.

London was emptying after the Regent's Fête and there was no possible reason for waiting until the autumn before they got married.

The Fête, to which so many people had looked forward, had been to Alexia's mind of so very little importance compared to Letty's wedding that she had found it hard to be as impressed as she should have been.

Two thousand invitations, as Mrs. Featherstone had learnt, had been despatched.

"Some," the Marquis remarked with a smile, "to people who were no longer living!"

The guests were invited for nine o'clock but it was difficult to reach Carlton House because Pall Mall, St. James's Street, and the Haymarket were blocked with carriages.

The Marquis, as the party were received in the Hall by various members of the household, had then proceeded to where the Regent himself stood waiting in a room hung with blue silk and decorated with golden fleur-de-lys.

This was because the Fête was given ostensibly in honour of the exiled Royal Family of France, and Alexia was presented to the *Ducs* de Berri, de Bourbon, and d'Angoulême, the Prince de Condé, and Louis XVI's only surviving child, the *Duchesse* d'Angoulême.

It was difficult, however, not to be blinded by the magnificence of their host, who eclipsed all his guests.

Wearing the uniform of Field-Marshal, a rank to which he had long aspired but from which his father had barred him for so long, he was sporting all his medals besides the glittering Star of the Order of the Garter and a splendid argrette.

Because the Marquis and the Dowager Marchioness were of such importance they sat down to dinner with two hundred of the Regent's most honoured friends beneath lanterns fixed to the fan-vaulted ceiling of the Gothic Conservatory.

There was so much to look at and so many important people to identify that Alexia found it hard to remember afterwards what she had eaten, although she was told that the dinner was superlative and even received the approval of the Marquis!

What fascinated her was that in front of the Regent on the table was a miniature fountain whose waters flowed in a silver-bedded stream to the right and to the left of him.

The stream was bounded by mossy banks, water-plants, and flowers, and tiny golden and silver fish swam through the arches of miniature bridges.

It was all impressive, but Alexia kept remembering the dozens of things that had to be done before Letty could be married two days later, and which only she could cope with because Letty's head was immersed in the clouds of love.

Now Letty was the Countess of Carthew and Alexia felt tears of joy prick her eyes as she threw the last pink petals from the basket she held in her hand.

"Good-bye! Good-bye!" Letty was crying.

Her eyes, vividly blue under a bonnet trimmed with ostrich-feathers of the same colour, seemed to shine with an inner light as she and the Earl drove away.

Alexia stood watching them until they were out of sight.

The white slipper which Peter had tied onto the back of the carriage was jumping up and down behind them and rose-petals were blowing off the closed hood of the carriage.

"It is so wonderful! It is like a fairy-story!" she said to herself.

Then a part of her mind saw Peter's new Tutor, a charming and intelligent young man, collecting him from among the other children who were being taken home by their parents.

There was an inordinate number of people to bid good-bye before finally Alexia found herself in the Library with only the Marquis and the Dowager Marchioness. It was the one room in the house which had not been used for the Reception.

The Marquis followed them and shut the door behind him.

"A glass of champagne, Mama?" he asked. "And then I think you should go to bed."

"I have every intention of doing so," the Dowager Marchioness replied. "It was a perfect wedding. You could not have organised it better, dearest, but I am a trifle fatigued."

"I am sure you must be," the Marquis said. "And now that Letty is settled, there is only one problem left for you."

"A problem?" the Dowager Marchioness asked. "And what is that?"

"The date on which Alexia and I should get married!" the Marquis replied.

For a moment there was complete and absolute silence while both Alexia and his mother looked at him in stupefaction.

Then the Dowager Marchioness said:

"Do you mean ... ? Oh, Chilton, my dearest boy, this is what I have prayed for!"

She put out her hands towards her son and he bent and kissed her cheek.

"I thought it would meet with your approval, Mama."

"My approval!" the Dowager Marchioness exclaimed.

She turned towards Alexia.

"You are exactly the wife I have wanted for my son," she said, "and the daughter I have ... wanted for ... myself."

There were tears in her eyes and her voice broke on the words.

"What I suggest, Mama," the Marquis said in his quiet voice, "is that you go upstairs and get into bed. After you have had something to eat and Alexia and I have dined downstairs, we will come and talk to you and make plans."

"I have never been so happy in my whole life!" the Dowager Marchioness exclaimed.

She kissed Alexia as the Marquis gave her his arm and led her out of the room and across the Hall to the bottom of the stairs, where her maid was waiting for her.

Alexia stood absolutely still when they had left her, feeling as if her feet were rooted to the ground, and yet the room was swimming dizzily round her.

It could not be true! She must have dreamt what the Marquis had said, and yet he had said it.

She had seen so little of him since they had returned from Dover because she had been completely preoccupied every day and almost every night with Letty's wedding.

Yet in her heart she had been content because he was there, because she was near him.

She knew too that he was triumphantly pleased with himself in having found exactly the right husband for Letty and solved that problem once and for all.

Sometimes when she could not sleep at night Alexia remembered that the moment when she must return to Bedfordshire was getting nearer and nearer.

The knowledge oppressed her, as it would mean she would not see the Marquis again.

Anticipating the misery of that moment when she must say good-bye, she treasured every glance she had of him, every word he spoke to her, repeating and re-repeating them to herself when she was alone.

"I love him!" she said despairingly over and over again into the darkness.

"I love him, Mama!" she had said in her prayers, "but what can I do about it?"

"I love him!" she had said as she touched the things in the house because they belonged to him.

The Marquis came into the room, shut the door, and stood looking at her.

Alexia's eyes seemed to fill her whole face.

Then quite simply, without words, he held out his arms.

Chapter Seven

For a moment Alexia felt as if she could not move.

Then there were wings on her feet and she ran towards the Marquis. As he put his arms round her and her face was upturned to his, his mouth came down on hers.

She knew this was what she had prayed, yearned, and craved for, and it was even more wonderful than she had thought it could be.

She had not imagined a kiss could make her feel as if a streak of sunlight ran through her body, making her pulsatingly alive.

It was so rapturous, so perfect, that she thought the angels she had heard singing at Letty's wedding were all round them, and the wonder of the Marquis's lips were part of the music, the beauty, and everything she had thought was out of reach.

It might have been a minute or a century before he raised his head and looked down at her.

She quivered against him and after a moment she said almost incoherently:

"Is . . . is this . . . true?"

"If you mean is it true that I intend to marry you," the Marquis answered. "I have discovered that I cannot contemplate life without you, and I am quite certain, my darling, that you cannot manage without me."

He pulled her a little closer to him and said:

"You have given me so many problems to solve, of which the most important is yourself. Now I have a solution to that as well."

There was a note of happiness in his voice that Alexia had never heard before. Then as if she was afraid to say it aloud she whispered:

"Please ... kiss me again ... in case I ... wake up."

* * *

The Marchioness of Osminton walked across the lawn hand in hand with her husband.

In the white gown she had worn for her wedding she looked not only lovely but so ethereal that the Marquis felt she might be part of the mist that was rising from the lake.

But Alexia looked at him with an expression of love in her grey eyes which told him she was real and very human.

To Alexia it was an irrepressible joy to realise that at last they were alone together after a day that had been filled with so many wonderful things which she knew she would always remember.

They had been married in the little grey Church which was just outside the gates of the Castle, and it had been a very different wedding from Letty's.

The congregation consisted only of the Marquis's relations and very close friends who lived in the immediate neighbourhood.

There had been no-one Alexia knew well to give her away, so she had walked up the aisle on the Marquis's arm.

The clergyman who had married them was the old Vicar of the Parish, who had known the Marquis ever since he was a small boy.

There was no choir, and yet it seemed to Alexia as if not only the angels were present at her marriage but also her father and mother.

When the Marquis made his vows in a deep voice

139

which told her that he was moved by the beautiful words, Alexia felt that she gave him not only her heart, which he possessed already, but also her soul.

"I love you!" she wanted to say.

They were the words she had repeated over and over again not only to him but in her prayers.

These were a paean of thanksgiving to God for having sent her a man who was so wonderful that she could still hardly believe she would not wake up and find that outside the window there was only the flat, dull countryside of Bedfordshire.

They had gone back from the Church to have a family banquet in the huge baronial Dining-Room where the ancestors of the Mintons looked down at them with what Alexia hoped were approving eyes.

The Marquis made a speech which made them all laugh, and then the guests drank the health of the bride and bridegroom, and Peter, who was tasting champagne for the first time in his life, declared in disgust that he much preferred lemonade.

Letty had come to the wedding from her new home in Oxfordshire, looking so radiantly happy that Alexia knew that never again would her younger sister be one of her problems.

"Being married is so marvellously exciting, Alexia," she said. "I know you will find it as thrilling as I do."

After luncheon was finished, quite late in the afternoon, Alexia and the Marquis said good-bye to their guests and lastly to the Dowager Marchioness.

She was taking Peter and his Tutor back to stay with her until their honeymoon was over.

The small boy was torn between the excitement of driving across country to a new place and leaving behind the horse the Marquis had given him.

"You must talk to Pegasus every day, Alexia," he said solemnly, "and tell him I am thinking of him."

"I will do that," Alexia had said with a smile.

Peter had hugged her, then flung his arms round the Marquis's legs.

"I will come back soon and help you with all your horses," he promised.

"That is very kind of you," the Marquis replied.

Alexia watched anxiously. She was afraid that the Marquis might think Peter a nuisance.

But he picked him up in his arms and put him on the back of one of the horses which were between the shafts of the carriage in which the Dowager Marchioness was to travel home.

"That will keep him out of mischief until Mama leaves," the Marquis remarked with a smile.

"I think," the Dowager Marchioness said before she left, "that with the exception of my own wedding-day, this has been the happiest day of my life!"

She looked up at her son with laughter in her eyes and added:

"I used to tell you when you were small that your mother knew best, and now you must admit that when I insisted on chaperoning those dear girls, much against your wishes, I was right."

"You were absolutely right, Mama," the Marquis answered, "and I vow, here and now, never to argue with you again!"

The Dowager Marchioness laughed.

"That is a vow I am quite certain you will not keep, but you know, my dearest boy, that if you had searched the whole wide world you could not have found a more perfect wife than Alexia."

"I did search the world for her," the Marquis answered, "and became completely convinced that she did not in fact exist!"

The Dowager Marchioness had driven away, but Peter, instead of sitting beside her, was up on the box beside the coachman, so that he could pretend he was driving.

When they had waved them out of sight, Alexia and the Marquis had gone to the great barn where those who worked on the estate were being entertained.

141

There were huge barrels of beer and cider and
everyone's smiling face looked pink and shining not
only with the heat but from the amount they had eaten
and drunk.

Here the Marquis made another speech and was
applauded until the very rafters of the barn seemed to
shake with the sound of it.

Afterwards they had returned to the Castle, which
now seemed in contrast very quiet.

But Alexia felt that the atmosphere was filled
with the impression of those who had lived there in the
past and who had carried on the family name.

She was sure they welcomed her and as she
moved through the flower-filled rooms she felt already that she belonged.

The Marquis came to her side as she stood in the
magnificent Salon.

"I think you must be tired, my precious," he
said, "but I have something to show you, and I
have waited all day for this moment."

She looked up at him enquiringly and he took
her by the hand and led her through one of the open
windows and out into the garden.

The sun had sunk in a blaze of glory and now
there was only the last touch of crimson behind the
great trees in the Park.

Overhead, the translucence of day was being encroached upon by the stable of the night and the first
pale evening star glittered over the ancient, great stone
tower which was all that remained of the original Castle.

There was the sound of the last rooks going to
roost and the fragrance of the flowers was heavy on
the still air.

After they had walked a little way in silence
the Marquis said:

"What is worrying you?"

"How do you know that I am worrying?" Alexia
asked.

"I can feel it," the Marquis answered, "and I do

not even have to look in your eyes, my beautiful darling, to know what you are thinking."

Alexia did not answer and he said with an amused note in his voice:

"Have you another problem for me?"

"Not . . . really a . . . problem."

"Tell me!" he commanded.

Alexia drew a little closer to him and her fingers tightened on his.

"I was . . . thinking," she said after a moment, "how magnificent all this is . . . how much you have given me . . . and how incredibly . . . fortunate I am."

She paused but the Marquis did not speak, for he knew she had not finished what she had to say.

"I . . . I was wondering how I could make you understand that even if you were of no . . . consequence whatsoever . . . if you possessed nothing . . . I would still . . . love you overwhelmingly and completely."

The Marquis heard the throb of sincerity in her voice and when he spoke his voice had deepened.

"I will answer that question a little later," he said, "and you shall prove your love, my precious, as you want to do."

As he spoke they had reached the end of the lawn which sloped upwards towards the great belt of trees which made a background for the Castle like a protective shield.

There were some steps rising at the side of a small cascade of water which ran over rocks into a marble pool.

Still holding Alexia's hand, the Marquis drew her up the steps and she found at the top of them there was a platform on which there was a seat beneath an exquisite statue of Diana the Huntress.

Because she knew the Marquis wished it Alexia sat down, then looked back the way they had come.

Immediately below them was the Castle, an architectural triumph of turrets and towers, roofs and chimneys silhouetted against the sky.

Beyond it was the silver lake with its black and

white swans, and beyond again the huge Park where the spotted deer rested in the shadows of the ancient trees.

It was so lovely that Alexia knew why the Marquis had brought her here.

He was watching the expression on her face, as he said:

"Every evening when I am living at the Castle I have always come here to look at this view, which to me is the most perfect in the world. Although I told myself it was complete, I always knew, though I would not admit it, that something was missing. It was you!"

Alexia raised her face to his and said:

"Everything about you is . . . so perfect, so beautiful . . . which was why I thought . . . you should have . . . married Letty."

The Marquis put his arm round her and drew her a little nearer.

"While I think that Letty is the most beautiful girl I have ever seen," he said, "she did not creep into my heart as you did when you first came into the Library in London."

"Is that . . . what I did?"

"You became a part of my heart," the Marquis replied, "although I would not admit it even to myself. But I wanted to help you, I wanted to protect you, which is something I had never felt before about any other woman."

Alexia felt a little pang of jealousy, thinking of all the beautiful women there had been in his life, but the Marquis went on:

"Then, when I knew you better, my mind was captivated by yours. I suppose I had never expected a woman to think seriously as you do on social and political questions, which have always been left to men."

"You do not . . . mind my being interested in . . . such things?" Alexia asked.

"It will help and inspire me to make a greater effort in that direction than I have done in the past."

She gave a little murmur of pleasure, and the Marquis went on:

"Having captivated my heart and my mind, my lovely wife, there is also something else which is a little harder to explain."

Alexia looked at him enquiringly and the Marquis said:

"I was thinking in Church today when we were married that you were like the lilies that were arranged on the altar. I have never felt that about any other woman with the exception of my mother."

Alexia clasped her hands together as she said:

"You are making me ... afraid that I will ... fail you. You are so ... clever and so wise ... and I ... ignorant about so ... many things."

"About what in particular?" the Marquis enquired.

Alexia turned her face away from him so that he could only see her profile silhouetted against the green of the surrounding trees.

The Marquis's eyes rested on her straight, aristocratic little nose, and on her firm chin, which had so much character in it.

Then he lingered on the softness of her curved lips, knowing they had never been touched by any man but himself.

She was everything, he thought, that he wanted to find in his wife, yet he had imagined he was asking too much, and that no human being could ever possibly fulfill the ideal that was enshrined within his imagination.

"What are you trying to tell me?" he asked aloud.

There was silence until in a low voice Alexia replied:

"I was thinking ... when we were in the Castle, that it is so ... large that there should be ... children to run about the Galleries ... and perhaps slide down the bannisters."

The Marquis did not speak and after a moment she said:

"I . . . know your mother longs for you to have a son . . . but although you have been so . . . kind and understanding to P-Peter . . . I thought perhaps you did not . . . like children."

Her voice was hesitating and the Marquis knew she was finding it difficult to say such things to him, and yet she sought the truth.

"Once, before I knew you," he answered, "I thought that children might disturb my well-organised life and perhaps be destructive, but now, because I love you, my darling, I can think of nothing more wonderful than to see you holding my son in your arms."

"Supposing . . . it was a . . . girl?"

"In that case," the Marquis replied, "we should obviously have to try again!"

There was a faint hint of laughter in his voice, but Alexia did not turn her head and he knew that something was still troubling her.

"Tell me," he said gently.

"You say I am . . . intelligent," Alexia answered, "and so you will think it very . . . foolish and ignorant of me . . . but I am not . . . sure . . . quite how one has a . . . baby."

The Marquis did not speak and she went on in a shy little voice:

"I thought I . . . ought to talk to Letty before she got married . . . but, as Mama is dead, there is . . . nobody I could ask to explain such things to me. Was it very remiss of me to have . . . remained silent?"

"I think, since we both saw today how happy Letty obviously is," the Marquis replied, "that James has made good your deficiency in that respect."

As he spoke, he thought that in comparing Alexia to a lily he had been even more perceptive than he had imagined.

He had for so long associated with sophisticated women who belonged to the raffish and rather fast set that surrounded the Regent at Carlton House that he had forgotten, if he had ever thought of it, that there were girls as pure and innocent as Alexia.

But in his soul he knew that this was what he had always wanted in his wife.

That she was looking away from him as she spoke because she was shy was, he found, so alluring, so fascinating, that for a moment his emotions seemed to overwhelm him.

He put his fingers under Alexia's small chin and turned her face round to his.

"I love you, my darling!" he said. "I love you so overwhelmingly, so completely, that it is going to take me a lifetime to tell you how much you mean to me."

"I love you . . . too!" Alexia murmured. "But there do not seem to be enough words in which to . . . express it."

"I told you your vocabulary was limited," the Marquis said with a smile, "but mine contains a word that I do not think I have spoken to anyone since I was a small boy, and then only to my mother."

Alexia looked at him questioningly and he said:

"You are part of my soul. That is what I want to tell you. My heart, my mind, and my soul belong to you, and therefore you fill my world, my whole existence, now and for eternity."

"Oh . . . Chilton!"

Alexia could hardly breathe his name, and he saw her grey eyes fill with tears.

"I am so . . . happy I want to . . . cry," she whispered, "so happy that it seems too overwhelming for me to understand. I only know that I . . . love you!"

"That is what I want you to tell me," the Marquis said.

She put her head against his shoulder.

"What I need are words . . . words to explain that when you . . . kiss me . . . when you . . . touch me, it is like being lifted up into the very . . . heart of the sun."

The Marquis pressed his lips against her forehead but he did not interrupt and she went on:

"I feel . . . the heat of the sun is in you . . . and in me, and it seems to . . . glow and intensify almost like a fire."

"And then?" the Marquis questioned.

"It is so difficult to . . . explain," Alexia said. "I do not want you to . . . stop kissing me . . . I want you to kiss me . . . more and more . . . and for me to be close . . . so close to you that I am part of you and you are . . . part of me."

The Marquis drew in his breath.

There was a touch of passion underlying Alexia's words, which she did not understand, but he did.

He stood up and drew her to her feet.

"We will be closer, my precious, so close that I can make you understand that you are mine completely and absolutely, and we are indivisible."

As he spoke he pulled her into his arms and his lips sought hers.

He kissed her at first as if she was something infinitely precious and sacred and he was afraid to frighten her.

Then, as he felt her press herself closer to him and he knew that he had awakened the heat of the sun within her, his lips became more passionate, more demanding.

The dusk of the night enveloped them, and the stars gleaming overhead seemed part of the magic in their hearts.

Then, in a voice so deep and unsteady that it seemed strange even to himself, the Marquis said:

"Let us go home, my darling wife, and I will solve your last problem not with words but with love."

ABOUT THE AUTHOR

BARBARA CARTLAND, the world's most famous romantic novelist, who is also an historian, playwright, lecturer, political speaker and television personality, has now written over 200 books. She has also had many historical works published and has written four autobiographies as well as the biographies of her mother and that of her brother Ronald Cartland, who was the first Member of Parliament to be killed in the last war. This book has a preface by Sir Winston Churchill. Barbara Cartland has sold 80 million books over the world, more than half of these in the U.S.A. She broke the world record in 1975 by writing twenty books, and her own record in 1976 with twenty-one. In private life, Barbara Cartland, who is a Dame of the Order of St. John of Jerusalem, has fought for better conditions and salaries for Midwives and Nurses. As President of the Royal College of Midwives (Hertfordshire Branch), she has been invested with the first Badge of Office ever given in Great Britain, which was subscribed to by the Midwives themselves. She has also championed the cause for old people and founded the first Romany Gypsy Camp in the world. Barbara Cartland is deeply interested in Vitamin Therapy and is President of the British National Association for Health.

A DUEL WITH DESTINY by BARBARA CARTLAND

The Marquis of Swayne is injured in a carriage accident and is carried to the house of the local physician. Here he is nursed by Rowena, oldest of a surprisingly beautiful family. The Marquis learns that Doctor Winsford, dedicated to his profession, is so generous to his poorer patients that his children suffer. He falls in love with Rowena, and she with him, and he offers her his protection.

How Rowena, horrified and disillusioned by such a suggestion, fights against the Marquis's charm and determination, how she tries to defeat him in a battle of wills and fails is told in this book by Barbara Cartland.

0 552 10549 X – 95p

PUNISHMENT OF A VIXEN by BARBARA CARTLAND

Tyrone Strome returns from a mission of great diplomatic importance to find his nephew is breaking his heart over an American heiress. He overhears Nevada Van Arden being extremely cruel and decides she is one of the most unpleasant women he has encountered.

On meeting her he finds she is very beautiful and hopelessly spoilt. To help his sister he abducts Nevada and takes her in his yacht to Morocco. How he punishes her, how they encounter danger and how beyond the desert they find the secret valley which is a second Garden of Eden is told in this book by Barbara Cartland.

0 552 10602 X – 95p

TOUCH A STAR by BARBARA CARTLAND

From Barbara Cartland comes the engrossing story of Lina, spirited young daughter of the Earl of Wallingham, who, escaping from an arranged marriage, applies for the post of a lady's maid- and finds herself involved in a plot to dupe a French roue - The Duc de Saverne ...

0 552 11969 5 - 95p

THE SECRET OF THE GLEN by BARBARA CARTLAND

From Barbara Cartland, one of the most romantic and internationally famous writers, comes a tale, set against the horror of the Highland Clearances, of an orphan girl who won the heart of a Clan Chieftain.

0 552 10228 8 - 95p

A PORTRAIT OF LOVE by BARBARA CARTLAND

From Barbara Cartland, comes an exciting new story about the beautiful but impoverished Fedora Colwyn, who plans to help her sick father pay off the family debts but instead finds herself implicated in a murder.

0 552 11876 1 – 95p

A SELECTION OF BARBARA CARTLAND
TITLES AVAILABLE IN CORGI PAPERBACK

WHILE EVERY EFFORT IS MADE TO KEEP PRICES LOW, IT IS SOMETIMES NECESSARY TO INCREASE PRICES AT SHORT NOTICE. CORGI BOOKS RESERVE THE RIGHT TO SHOW AND CHARGE NEW RETAIL PRICES ON COVERS WHICH MAY DIFFER FROM THOSE ADVERTISED IN THE TEXT OR ELSEWHERE.

THE PRICES SHOWN BELOW WERE CORRECT AT THE TIME OF GOING TO PRESS (MAY '82).

All these books are available at your bookshop or newsagent, or can be ordered direct from the publisher. Just tick the titles you want and fill in the form below.

CORGI BOOKS, Cash Sales Department, P.O. Box 11, Falmouth, Cornwall.

Please send cheque or postal order, no currency.

Please allow cost of book(s) plus the following for postage and packing:

U.K. Customers – Allow 45p for the first book, 20p for the second book and 14p for each additional book ordered, to a maximum charge of £1.63.

B.F.P.O. and Eire – Allow 45p for the first book, 20p for the second book plus 14p per copy for the next 7 books, thereafter 8p per book.

Overseas Customers – Allow 75p for the first book and 21p per copy for each additional book.

NAME (Block Letters) ....

ADDRESS ....

....